Billings turned t[...], intending to complete the spelling of PRESENT. And then everything went wrong. He forgot about his right ankle, and he twisted it when he tried to move his right leg into a more comfortable position on the time sled. His reaction to the sudden surge of pain was disastrous, for when he attempted to alleviate the pain by straightening his leg, he kicked the cable that led from the batteries to the photon scrambler. There was a jar, a lurch and a blink of blackness; then daylight again, and a strange new landscape.

Looking at it, Billings was certain it didn't belong in the Ninth century.

He was just as certain it didn't belong in the Twenty first.

He wasn't even sure it belonged on Earth.

ROBERT F. YOUNG, born in New York state in 1915, is best known as a writer of short stories. His tales have been appearing in many magazines since 1953, including most of the sf and fantasy titles such as *Fantasy and Science Fiction*, *Analog*, *Galaxy*, *Amazing*, and *Venture*. Two such collections have been published in hardcover book form, *A Glass of Stars* and *The Worlds of Robert F. Young*. Recent novels have included *The Last Yggdrasil* and *Eridahn*.

THE
VIZIER'S SECOND DAUGHTER

Robert F. Young

DAW Books, Inc.
Donald A. Wollheim, Publisher
1633 Broadway, New York, N.Y. 10019

PUBLISHED BY
THE NEW AMERICAN LIBRARY
OF CANADA LIMITED

DAW Collectors' Book No. 616

First Printing, February 1985

2 3 4 5 6 7 8 9

PRINTED IN CANADA
COVER PRINTED IN U.S.A.

Prologue

To see her reclining there on the Sultan's couch, her left arm resting on the cushioned back, her bloomered legs drawn up beneath her, it was difficult to believe she was an animanikin and not the real Sheherazade. She was so lifelike that Mark Billings, if he hadn't known better, would have sworn that she was flesh and blood.

The strains of Rimsky-Korsakov's *Scheherazade* sounded in the background as she began to relate "The Story of the Porter and the Ladies of Baghdad." The Sultan, whose name was Shahriyar, seemed to be listening to her every word, even though he was an animanikin too. A silver crown rested upon his head, and he wore a white silk gown and a crimson cummerbund.

Other people crowded against Billings as he

stood enthralled just behind the velvet cord
that separated the Thousand and One Nights
exhibit from the museum floor. Upon a dais
behind the crowd a TV team began relaying the
exhibit's debut into millions and millions of
American living rooms.

The Sultan's bedchamber had been meticu-
lously copied from holographs of the original.
In the background, slender columns supported
the bases of bell-shaped arches. A brazier hung
on burnished brass chains from the high ceiling,
and the rich tapestries that curtained the couch
were drawn back at the sides with golden draw
cords with tassels as black as Sheherazade's
hair.

"There was a man of the city of Baghdad,
who was unmarried, and he was a porter; and
one day as he sat in the market reclining against
a crate, there accosted him a female wrapped
in an izar of the manufacture of El-Mosil, com-
posed of gold-embroidered silk, with a border
of lace at each end, who raised her face-veil
and displayed beneath it a pair of black eyes
with lids bordered by long lashes, exhibiting a
tender expression and features of perfect beauty;
and she said with a sweet voice, 'Bring thy
crate, and follow me. . . .' "

Such a long, long sentence, Sheherazade, Billings thought. But in your day long sentences
were all the rage, as were tales within tales
within tales. But you told the Sultan only a

thousand and one, Sheherazade. There's still one more. It has to do with Jinn and ghuls and gold, with a magic carpet and a girl with violet eyes; with a land that was both legendary and real.

It also has to do with me.

He wished that he had stayed home. He should have known that even a glimpse into the past, however make-believe the scene might be, would bring everything back. Desperately he tried to hang on to the present, but he could not, and the centuries became a deep, dark well, and he fell through the darkness to the Sultan's palace where "The Story of the Vizier's Second Daughter" had begun. . . .

I

Enter Dunyzad

The seraglio had two guards—big black eunuchs wearing diaperlike loincloths and armed with yard-long scimitars. One was stationed a short distance down the lamplit corridor from the curtained doorway through which the girl Billings had followed from the Sultan's bedchamber had passed a quarter of an hour ago, and the other stood by the door.

Billings peered at them around the column behind which he was waiting to give his quarry a chance to fall asleep. His clothing, although not its material, was in tune with the times: a white melwatah, with a vest, a loose shirt and wide trousers underneath, and Persian slippers and a lightweight turban.

At length, certain that by this time the girl must be in dreamland, he pulled his icer from the holster sewn inside the left sleeve of his melwatah, leveled it at the eunuch standing between him and the doorway and quick-froze him. Then he ran forward and eased the man's descent to the floor.

Thus far since sneaking into the Sultan's palace he had attracted no attention, for at this hour of the morning only a few menials were abroad. Some of them had seen him, but apparently they had assumed he was a guest of the Sultan's who had gotten up when dawn's left hand was still in the sky. But now he had no choice but to reveal himself for the intruder he really was, for icers —the only type of weapon VIPPnappers were allowed to carry—were functional only at very short ranges, and he was much too far from the other guard to put him out of action.

The guard, who had been looking the other way, was as yet unaware of what had happened to his buddy. Billings moved swiftly down the corridor toward him, his slippered feet soundless on the carpeted floor. But before he came within range, the eunuch instinctively turned in his direction, and in a split second the man's scimitar was in his hand. Billings, knowing it would be useless to try to come up with a legitimate excuse for being in territory that was off-limits to all bona fide males except the Sultan himself and that it would be downright absurd to try to come up with one that would allow him to pass through the doorway, didn't slow his footsteps, and kept his icer pointed at the guard's chest.

"Know," the eunuch shouted, making several bloodcurdling passes with his scimitar, "that if you do not depart at once I will disembowel thee and throw thy entrails to the dogs!"

Billings increased his pace, fearful now that the guard would sound an alarm. But he did not; instead, openly contemptuous of Billings, he stepped forward and started to swing his scimitar in a vicious arc that, had it been completed, would have sliced Billings in half. But at this point Billings' icer transformed him into an icicle, or as close to one as it is possible for a human being to become without expiring, and he would have fallen flat on his face if Billings hadn't eased him down to the floor. The scimitar, which had slipped from the eunuch's fingers, made no sound when it landed on the carpet.

Parting the curtains, Billings stepped into the chamber beyond the doorway. He felt sorry for the two guards because of the discomfort they would experience when they thawed out, but a job was a job, and he intended to abduct the once-legendary raconteuse of *The Thousand and One Nights* regardless of how many human icicles he had to leave behind.

Actually he was only going to borrow her, and as soon as Big Pygmalion, Animanikins

Incorporated's electronic sorcerer, made an animated facsimile of her for the forthcoming Thousand and One Nights exhibit, he would bring her back. If all went well, he would deposit her within walking distance of the palace in less than an hour, ninth-century time. She would be shaken up, but no harm would have been done.

To the right of the doorway two canopied couches stood side by side, and on the nearer one, bathed in the gray dawnlight coming through a wide latticed window in the wall opposite the door, lay the figure of the girl. The recounting of her most recent tale must have exhausted her, for she had removed only her slippers and her kufiyeh and had gone to bed with the rest of her clothes on.

The other couch was empty. No doubt it was the Sultan's.

Billings holstered his icer and approached the girl. Her perfume touched his nostrils. No, it didn't merely touch them, it overwhelmed them. He identified it as nedd, a scent as popular in her day as *Jeu de Printemps, numéro cinq*, was in his. Oddly, he found the ancient perfume the more pleasing of the two, but it did not sway him from his purpose, and pulling a somni-sponge from an inside pocket in the right sleeve of his melwatah, he removed the plastic seal and held the sponge against the girl's nose and mouth. At once she awoke and

began to struggle, but the drug did its dirty
work in a matter of seconds, and presently she
went limp. Tossing the sponge aside, he picked
up her slippers and wedged them into the neck
of his melwatah and then swung the girl over
his shoulder. Marveling at how light she was,
he stepped back out into the corridor. And
right then and there his luck ran out, for whom
did he see hurrying toward the fallen guards
but Shahriyar himself!

It was true that Billings had never before seen
the Sultan in the flesh, but he had seen his
animanikin, for Shahriyar had already been VIPP-
napped and returned by Jed Morse, a veteran
VIPPnapper whose place Billings had taken
when Jed came down with the flu. Billings had
taken past-travel training and had been waiting
for months for Animanikins to call him, and if
he carried out his mission successfully he would
graduate from the supernumerary pool and be
hired on a full-time basis.

He hated Bluebeards and would have liked
nothing better than to have turned this one into
an icicle, even though the Historical Research
Team had learned that although Sheherazade
really had told the Sultan a thousand and one
tales, he had never beheaded any of his wives,
and therefore could not be classified as a Bluebeard. But he *looked* like a Bluebeard, and
Billings would gladly have given in to the temp-

tation if the Sultan, upon seeing him with the
girl slung over his shoulder, had not begun
shouting at the top of his voice for the other
palace guards, for his black slaves, for his
menials, for his Vizier and for the nearest wali.
Cornered, Billings did the only thing he could
do: he plunged back into the room, and with
the girl still slung over his shoulder, made a
beeline for the window.

Was the latticework wood or metal? he wondered. He kicked it, and the arabesques went
flying. Climbing up on the sill, he jumped down
into the courtyard below without even looking
to see how far he had to fall.

It was much farther than he had thought, and
when he landed he turned his right ankle. The
sprain wasn't a severe one, but it made walking
an ordeal and running an impossibility. He could
see the grove of date palms where he had hidden his time sled. The trees grew in the palace's
back yard, and to reach them he would have to
cut diagonally across the courtyard. He set forth
grimly, grimacing with every other step.

The whole palace was awake by this time.
The Sultan was leaning through the window
Billings had jumped from and was shouting at
the top of his voice, and guards with scimitars
and black slaves and menials armed with broom-
sticks and other makeshift weapons were pouring into the courtyard. To make matters worse,
about ten thousand dogs appeared from no-

where and began yapping around Billings' ankles, and to make them even worse, the somni-drug he had administered to the girl wore off and she began kicking and squirming and screaming, and pounding on his back with her fists. Some of the things she said made his ears burn. In ancient Arabic, which he had taken a crash course in, they didn't sound quite as bad as they would have in English, but they sounded bad enough, and if he had had a third hand and a long enough third arm he would have given her a few good wallops.

The guards and the menials and the black slaves began charging him, but neither their scimitars nor their makeshift weapons did them any good because they feared harming his captive, so he was able to ice them down indiscriminately. The courtyard began to take on the aspect of a statuary exhibition that a strong wind had just blown through. No question about it, when the Hunter of the East finally caught the Sultan's turret in a noose of light, he was going to have a king-sized defrosting job on his hands.

Reaching the grove, Billings made his way straight to his time sled. "Toboggan" would have been a better name for it, for despite its greater width, that was what it looked like. The seat was elevated, and beneath it was the photon scrambler, which was housed in a titanium cylinder. Behind the seat, bolted to the deck, were two big metal boxes. One contained tools and parts, the other camping equipment and rations and various other items a time traveler might need in the event of a major breakdown. In front of the seat, capped by the control board, were the anti-grav generator, the intra-era inertia regulator and the batteries.

The seat was more than wide enough for two. Plumping the girl down upon it, he secured her in place with one of the two safety belts, then sat down beside her and, after fastening the other belt around his hips, turned the altitude dial to 200 and depressed the hover button. Promptly the sled lifted, deftly avoiding the fronds of the palms, and came to a smooth stop two hundred feet above the ground.

Just as promptly the girl stopped struggling and screaming and stared over the edge of the sled at the tops of the palms. Then she turned and stared at him with eyes that the first rays of the rising sun revealed to be the color of violets. "A magic carpet!" she gasped.

This was exactly what Aloysius Smith, Animanikins' chief historical adviser, had told Billings an Arabian girl of the ninth century would say when she was borne aloft on a time sled. And Smith, who had done a paper on Arabian damsels, had also told Billings that if he wanted to keep his captive quiet he should pass himself off as an emir. Every ninth-century Arabian damsel, Smith had asseverated, secretly dreams of someday being carried off by an emir on a magic carpet. Even the wife of a Sultan? Billings had asked. *Especially* the wife of a Sultan, Smith had said learnedly.

So Billings said, "I am an emir."

For a while his captive just looked at him. Then she said, "I suppose you have come to bear me away."

Her voice was light and airy, and seemed invested with the tinkling of faraway bells. He handed her her slippers. "Yes, a long ways away."

Shouts and imprecations were rising faintly from the courtyard. Ignoring them, he took a good look at her after she put her slippers on. Her hair was black, and pulled back behind her ears and secured by a barrette. Her nose was straight and rounded at the end, and she had full cheeks, an expressive mouth and a rounded chin. Her violet eyes had no business being quite so large, any more than they had any business being blue. Except for a big ring on the middle finger of her left hand, she wore no jewels, unless you counted the barrette. Her melwatah had been cut short and came only to her hips. It was open, exposing her chest all the way down to the top of her bloomers which, while they came much higher than twenty-first-century bloomers did, barely hid her breasts. He saw then that she had next to none to hide.

It dawned on him finally that she was only about fifteen years old.

Fifteen years old and married to a king!

Well, he could accept the reality of that. In this day and age kings were not about to pick older women when they could have all the young ones they wanted, and could get away with it. But he had difficulty accepting the fact that she was the author of a thousand and one cliff-hangers, and it galled him to think that she had to sit night after night recounting them to a Bluebeard king who was old enough to be her father, and maybe even old enough to be her grandfather!

He wished he could take her away permanently, but he couldn't, of course. Very Important Past Persons belonged in the past, just as ordinary past persons did. All he could do was take her on a round trip to the future, and this was tantamount to doing nothing at all.

His helplessness distressed him, and he knew that the sooner he got the job over with, the better. Activating the photon scrambler, he started to punch out P R E S E N T on the trans-era keyboard. Then, when he got as far as the R, a thought struck him. No, it didn't strike him—it clobbered him. He returned his eyes to his captive. "You are Sheherazade, aren't you?"

"Of course I am not. I am her sister, Dunyzad. She is the Sultan's Vizier's first daughter, I am his second."

Billings sat there stunned.

"Surely you did not come to bear Sheherazade away," Dunyzad said.

"No, no, no. no."

"Shahriyar would be quite furious if such had been your intention. He is quite madly in love with her. Do you know," Dunyzad went on, "I am quite pleased that you came for me. I like living in the Sultan's palace, but he is very strict and will never let me go anywhere alone. He does not trust me. But you must know how strict he is, or you would not have carried me off in the way that you did. He looks upon me the way he would look upon a daughter, if he had one. I would not be living in his palace were it not for my sister. When the Sultan married her she tricked him into taking me along too. She entertains him nightly by telling him stories, and each night, in order to get her started, I have to sit by their couch and say, 'By Allah, O my sister, relate to us a story to beguile the waking hour of our night.' And then she tells the story, only she does not tell all of it, she breaks off at the most exciting part and makes the Sultan wait till the next night for the second part. But I think she can get along without me for a while. As soon as we reach your palace, though, I must send her and the Sultan a message assuring them that no harm has befallen me and that I have not been visited by the terminator of delights and the separator of companions. If you wish to make me your bride, you will have to get the Sultan's permission, and my father's as well."

"Sure," Billings said.

"But I am aware of course," she went on, her eyes a deeper violet than before, "that this may not be your intention. Just because an emir bears a girl away on a magic carpet that is not a positive indication he is in love with her. Love is too elusive to be thus easily captured, and only time will tell whether it will become part of our hopes and dreams."

"How do you know," Billings asked weakly, "that I really *am* an emir?"

"How could you not be one when you own a magic carpet? Besides which," she added, "you *look* like an emir."

Perhaps he did, but he didn't feel like one. VIPPnapping Sheherazade's kid sister instead of Sheherazade herself! How in the world could he have made such a stupid mistake!

But in all fairness to himself, it hadn't been completely stupid. How could he have known that the girl he had followed from the Sultan's bedchamber to the seraglio wasn't Sheherazade? He had only had lamplight to go by, and the Historical Research Team had never showed him a holograph of Dunyzad, nor told him that the two girls slept in the same bedroom.

But the fact remained that he had goofed, and for a while things looked dark indeed for his future. Presently, though, he saw a ray of light. Animanikins, Inc. would need an animanikin of Dunyzad too, or the Thousand and One Nights Exhibit wouldn't be authentic. So the trip wouldn't be a wasted one. He would simply take Dunyzad to the future, explain his mistake to the Curator, and then, when he brought her back, he would snatch Sheherazade. It would take some doing after the ruckus he had just caused, but he was certain he could bring it off.

He turned toward the control board again, intending to complete the spelling of P R E S E N T. And then everything went wrong. He forgot about his right ankle, and he twisted it when he tried to move his right leg into a more comfortable position. His reaction to the sudden surge of pain was disastrous, for when he attempted to alleviate the pain by straightening his leg, he kicked the cable that led from the batteries to the photon scrambler. There was a jar, a lurch and a blink of blackness; then daylight again, and a strange new landscape.

Looking at it, Billings was certain it didn't belong in the ninth century.

He was just as certain it didn't belong in the twenty-first.

He wasn't even sure it belonged on Earth.

II

The 'Efrit

Below the sled, where a moment ago the grove of date palms had been, was a small oasis. But it resembled no oasis Billings had ever seen. The palm trees grew in perfect circles, one circle just within the other, and in the center of the innermost circle stood a tree much larger than the rest. On most of the treetops watermelon-sized fruit grew in clusters, and on the tops of the fruitless trees were large clusters of yellow blossoms. He deduced—correctly, as later events proved—that some of the fruit had been picked and that more was being grown.

To the north and the west and the south a desert dotted with similar oases stretched away to what appeared to be low-lying hills. To the east, the direction in which the sled was pointed, the desert gave way to hills backgrounded by a low range of mountains. The sun—the standard for his orientation—had just winked into sight above a col between two of the peaks.

In the foreground there was a small blue lake, and beyond it a white, domelike structure broke the monotony of the oases. Other domes were visible far to the north and the west and the south.

He looked at Dunyzad, curious to see how the abrupt change of scene had affected her. She didn't seem to be in the least upset. In fact, the expression on her face was one of fascination.

He was both relieved and annoyed. She should have been scared. He was.

After deactivating the photon scrambler, he examined the cable which he had accidentally kicked. Three of its strands had pulled free from the scrambler's connection box. Reconnecting them would pose no problem, but before he traveled into the future he would first have to get back to where he had been, and this posed a real problem.

The sun, at least, was in approximately the same place in the sky, and this afforded him some measure of relief. But its light did not seem quite right. It had a faint reddish cast. Stealing a swift glance at the sun itself, he saw that it, too, had a faint reddish cast. It also seemed to be bigger.

But was it the sun? For all he knew, it might

be a different star. The photon scrambler, react-
ing eccentrically to a partial loss of power,
might have catapulted the sled into a different
part of the universe. The only other tentative
conclusion he could come to was that the scrambler had somehow carried the sled into the far
future.

Tonight he would be able to tell which conclusion was correct. Not from the constellations,
for the constellations of the far future would be
no more familiar to his eyes than those in the
sky of an alien planet, but from the absence or
presence of the moon. "Last night," when it
had risen above the Sultan's palace, it had been
full. If it appeared tonight in any of its visible
phases, he would know that he and Dunyzad
were still on Earth

Someone was tugging on the sleeve of his melwatah, and he realized that Dunyzad had said
something to him. He looked at her. "You have
yet to inform me," she repeated, "in what manner you wish me to address you."

"My real name's Mark, but most people call
me Bill."

"You wish me to call you *Bill*?"

"Bill will be fine."

"Such a strange name for an emir!"

"If you'd rather, you can call me Mark."

"No. I like Bill better. How big is your palace,
Bill?"

Her inference that he had one was only natural in view of the fact that he'd told her he was an emir, so he continued to let the assumption stand. In fact, he made it worse by saying his palace was good-sized. Actually, he lived in a mobile home next to a junkyard. When he had worked his way through college he had majored in computer programming, but so had just about everybody else in his generation, and there were far more programmers on the job market than there were computers for them to program. There were plenty of openings in other, less sophisticated fields however, and rather than go home and sponge off his parents he had gotten a job as dishwasher and rented a mobile home. Finally, sick of being as poor as a churchmouse, he had put in his application at Animanikins, Inc. and had taken pasttravel training and become part of the supernumerary pool.

"Is it bigger than the Sultan's?" Dunyzad asked.

"Let's forget about my palace for a while. I've got more important things to think about."

Suddenly she seized his arm and pointed across the lake. "Look, Bill—a Jinni!"

He looked in the direction she was pointing, but all he saw was what appeared to be a whirling pillar of sand. He said as much. "But how can sand whirl," Dunyzad asked, "when there is no wind? No, it is a Jinni. And an evil one, too, I think. An 'Efrit at least. Perhaps even a Marid."

He had to admit there was no wind. As a matter of fact, there was not even a breeze. As though to confound reality further, the pillar, after whirling down to the edge of the lake, began whirling across the water. Since it seemed to be headed for the oasis, he decided that whatever it was, his best bet would be to stay out of its path, so after activating the intra-era inertia regulator he flew the sled on a diagonal course to another oasis about half a mile away and landed on the grassy apron that surrounded it. He turned to Dunyzad then, ready with the reassuring words which he felt the abrupt flight from oasis to oasis demanded.

He did not utter them. She was sitting up straight on the seat and her eyes were sparkling and she looked like a kid who had just had her first ride on a roller coaster and could not wait for the second. "Why did you come down, Bill? Come, let us fly some more!"

"You should be scared out of your wits!"

"Why should I be?"

"You can't possibly have ridden on one of these things before."

"No, but I have dreamed of riding on a magic carpet hundreds of times, and dreaming of doing something is almost the same thing as doing it."

"I'll bet you've never even seen a magic carpet before."

"No, I never have. But I have always known there were such things. Come, let us fly all the way up to the top of the sky!"

"Not right now."

He unfastened his seat belt and stepped gingerly down to the ground. When he pulled off his right slipper he saw that his ankle was beginning to swell. He pulled up his melwatah and got his jackknife out of one of the pockets of his trousers; then he sat down, removed his turban, partially unwound it and cut off a two-foot length of the material. By this time Dunyzad had managed to unfasten her own belt, and now she flew to his side. "I did not know you had hurt yourself, Bill!" She took the knife and the material away from him and bandaged the ankle herself. Then she forced his foot back into his slipper and told him to stand up. When he did so he found he could put all of his weight on his right foot without suffering the slightest pain, and a few tentative steps informed him that he could walk without limping.

He opened the toolbox, found a screwdriver, and reconnected the three strands of the cable. When he finished he replaced the screwdriver in the box. Dunyzad was staring at the mélange of objects it contained. "What are all those strange things, Bill?"

"Tools. Sometimes magic carpets break down and you have to fix them."

"Those little rods of metal. They look like they are lead."

"Solder." He used the English word. "But yes, I guess you could say lead, because that's what it mostly is."

"What is that little clay pot?"

"It's a self-heating crucible. If you need a lot of lead, you put some of the rods in and flick that little switch on the side, and they'll melt." He pointed to a little ladle. "You use that to dip it out with."

"Oh."

He closed the box. He saw that she had tipped her head to one side. "I can hear water bubbling, Bill."

He listened. Presently he heard the bubbling sound too. It came from within the oasis. "There must be a spring among the trees," Dunyzad said. "I am going to see."

He followed her into the oasis. They found not one spring but several—little pools of clear water with bubbles rising to the surface. They indicated that the oasis must be irrigated. Probably all the others were too. The white domes must be pumping stations.

Dunyzad had knelt down before one of the springs. *Don't drink any of the water!* he started to say, but she had already cupped some into her mouth. Oh well, he thought, and knelt down and cupped some into his. Accustomed as he was to twenty-first-century water, he thought for a moment that he was drinking champagne. This water could not poison anybody. He cupped some more of it into his mouth, wondering why he had not been poisoned long ago by water drawn from his own tap.

It was idyllic beneath the trees. He returned to the sled and brought back two boxes of rations. He opened a mini-can of corned beef and a mini-can of cheese for her and a mini-can of corned beef and a mini-can of cheese for himself and they ate breakfast sitting beside the spring.

Dunyzad marveled at the cheese. "Such wonderful goats you must have!"

"You can't beat them," Billings said.

A wind must have sprung up, for he could hear it as it hummed over the desert. Dunyzad was listening too. "It's nothing to worry about," Billings reassured her. "It's only the wind."

She shook her head. "No. If it was a wind the fronds of the trees would be waving, and they are still. It is a Jinni. Maybe the one we saw before or maybe a different one."

Her reprise made Billings mad. "If it's a Jinni," he demanded, "why aren't you afraid?"

"*Afraid!*" Indignation turned her eyes a bellflower blue. "It is the Jinn who should be afraid of me!" She raised her left hand so he could see the ring on her middle finger. "The seal is made of brass and iron, and iron, as you should know, Bill, is excessively dreaded by the Jinn. And the seal is exactly like the seal which Suleyman Ibn-Da'ud used to imprison the Jinn in brass bottles hundreds of years ago. With such a ring upon my finger, how could I possibly be afraid of a mere Jinni, or even an 'Efrit or a Marid?''

Billings gave the ring only a casual glance. "I still say that what we're hearing is the wind."

"Let us go and find out."

He followed her through the trees to the grassy apron. The humming had become much louder, and he saw why. The same pillar of sand they had seen before, or one just like it, was whirling toward the oasis. Gray and ominous, verging in places on black, and about ten feet high, it brought to mind a miniature tornado.

As he stared at it, it doubled its pace. Instinctively he drew his icer. "You see, Bill?" Dunyzad said. "You see?"

He saw all right. And he also saw that they were too far from the time sled to be able to reach it in time to do them any good. Not believing his eyes, he watched the pillar whirl right up to the edge of the apron and come to a stop. The humming faded away then, and the sand, if sand it was, began to coalesce. Presently he discerned a pair of huge splayed feet and a pair of grapnellike hands. At length he made out the creature's head. It brought to mind a big brass kettle turned upside down. The face came into focus. The eyes were like fanwheels, the nose resembled a squashed potato and the huge mouth was open, revealing two rows of tombstonelike teeth. As Billings stared, the rows ground together and a number of sparks shot forth.

He pointed the icer at the creature's midriff and put a protective arm around Dunyzad's shoulders. If the darn thing came any closer, he would turn it into a big icicle. But it came no closer. Instead, after grinding its teeth a few more times, it turned back into a miniature tornado and began circumventing the oasis. *Hum-hum-hum*, it went. *Hum-hum-hum*. He watched it till the trees hid it from view.

"It was an 'Efrit," Dunyzad said, "and it was spying on us."

He removed his arm from her shoulders. "What's the difference," he asked, less out of curiosity than from an effort to regain his aplomb, "between a Jinni and an 'Efrit?"

"You have never seen an 'Efrit before?"

"No."

"Nor a Marid?"

"No."

"Well both are Jinn, as you should know, Bill. But an 'Efrit is a powerful, evil Jinni, and a Marid an evil and even more powerful one. Some people believe that there are Sheytans too, and that they are the most powerful of all. But I do not think they exist."

"How did you know the Jinni we just saw was an 'Efrit?" Billings asked.

"From its face. Did you see how mean it was?"

"It was mean all right."

"But we had nothing to fear. The Jinn are helpless against the seal of Suleyman. I am glad, Bill," she went on, "that you chose to go through the Veil on the way to your palace, for I have always wanted to see the mountains of Kaf."

"The mountains of Kaf?"

She pointed toward the range of mountains that rose in the east. "Yes. Those mountains. They encircle the Earth."

"Dunyzad, do you know where we are?"

"Of course. We are in the land of the Jinn." She stared at him. "You did not know?"

He shook his head. "But why did you go through the Veil?" she asked, "if you did not know what was on the other side?"

"Dunyzad, I don't even know what the Veil is."

"Well no one knows exactly what it is. My knowledge of it is more extensive than that of most people because of something that happened to me when I was still living in my father's house." She looked up into his face with her violet eyes. "Would you like me to tell you about it?"

He could see she was just dying to. Well why not let her? he thought. If she could throw any light whatsoever upon their predicament, it would be more than welcome. "Go ahead, Dunny," he said.

"It is quite a long story, so I think we had better sit down. I do not believe the 'Efrit will be back."

He sat down on the grass and she sat down facing him. "I will begin at the very beginning," she said.

III

The Veil

"There came one day to the dwelling of my father the Vizier a poor fisherman who, for a mere kataif, offered to sell him a brass bottle which he had caught in his net and which was sealed with a lead stopper bearing the seal of our lord Suleyman. My father gave the poor man the pastry and accepted the bottle in return, and afterward placed it in a secluded part of the courtyard. When I saw it there early the next morning I went over and looked at it. My curiosity, which had been awakened, grew great when I picked the bottle up and found it to be excessively heavy. I then looked at the seal, but as I did not know its true nature as yet my curiosity was only further increased, and I went into the kitchen and obtained a knife and picked at the lead till I extracted the stopper. Immediately smoke came forth and ascended toward the sky and spread out over the face of the Earth. After a while it collected together and became condensed, and then it became agitated and was converted into an 'Efrit, whose head was in the clouds, while its feet rested upon the ground. Its head was like a dome, its hands were like winnowing forks, and its legs like masts. Its mouth resembled a cavern, its teeth were like stones, its nostrils like trumpets, and its eyes like lamps. It had disheveled and dust-colored hair. I was so terrified I did not know what to do.

"The moment it saw me, the 'Efrit exclaimed, 'There is no deity but God; Suleyman is the Prophet of God. O Prophet of God, slay me not, for I will never again oppose you in word, or rebel against you in deed!' 'O 'Efrit,' I said, 'do you say Suleyman is the Prophet of God? Suleyman has been dead a thousand and seven hundred years. What is your history and why were you imprisoned in this bottle?' When the 'Efrit heard these words, it said, 'There is no deity but God! Receive news, O damsel!' 'Of what?' I inquired, 'do you bring me news?' The 'Efrit answered, 'Of your being instantly put to death.' 'I do not understand,' I said. 'Why should you wish to kill me when I have just liberated you from your prison?' The 'Efrit answered, 'Choose what kind of death you wish me to inflict upon

you.' 'But what is my offense?' I asked. The
'Efrit replied, 'Hear my story, O damsel.' 'Tell
it then and be quick,' I said, for the arrogance
of the 'Efrit had made me furious.

" 'Know then,' it said, 'that I am one of the
heretical Jinn. I rebelled against Suleyman the
son of Da'ud; I and Sakir the Jinni; and he sent
me to his Vizier, Asaf the son of Barkhiya, who
came upon me forcibly and took me to Suleyman
and placed me before him. And when Suleyman
saw me, he offered up a prayer for protection
against me and exhorted me to embrace the
faith and to submit to his authority; but I refused,
upon which he called for this bottle and confined me in it and closed it upon me with the
leaden stopper, which he stamped with his
seal. He then gave orders to the good Jinn, who
carried me away and threw me into the sea.
There I remained a hundred years, and I said
in my heart, "Whosoever shall liberate me, I
shall enrich him forever." But the hundred years
passed over me and no one liberated me and I
entered upon another hundred years, and I said,
"Whosoever shall liberate me, I will open to
him the treasures of the earth." But no one did
so, and four hundred more years passed over
me, and I said, "Whosoever shall liberate me, I
will perform for him three wants." But still no
one liberated me. I then fell into a violent rage
and said within myself, "Whosoever shall liber-

ate me now, I will kill him, and only suffer him to choose in what manner he wishes to die." And lo, now you at last have liberated me, O damsel, and I have given you your choice in the manner in which you prefer to die.'

"When I heard this story I felt assured of my death. And then I thought, This is a Jinni and I am a damsel, and God has given me sound reason, and I said then to the 'Efrit, 'Before you kill me I would like to ask you one question. Will you answer it?' And the 'Efrit replied, 'Yes. Ask it and be brief.' I then said, 'How could you have fitted inside this bottle? It will not contain your hand or your foot—how then could it contain your whole body?' 'You do not believe I was in it?' asked the 'Efrit. 'No,' I answered, 'I will never believe until I see you pass inside.' 'I will show you!' the 'Efrit cried, and at once converted itself back into smoke, which rose into the sky and then became condensed and entered the bottle little by little until it was all enclosed. Quickly I snatched the leaden stopper and replaced it in the bottle's mouth. Then, calling out to the 'Efrit, I said, 'Choose in what manner you wish to die!' Upon hearing my words, the 'Efrit endeavored to escape, but I knew it could not, for now I understood the true nature of the seal. 'What will you do with me?' it cried. 'I am going to throw you back into the sea,' I said, 'and there

you shall remain until the hour of judgment.'
'No, no!' the 'Efrit cried. 'Liberate me, and for
my freedom I will tell you of the Veil which
divides the land of Men from the land of the
Jinn.' 'I have heard of the Veil,' I said, 'but I do
not understand it.' 'I will tell you about it and
explain its true nature the moment you have
liberated me,' said the 'Efrit. 'No,' I said, 'you
will tell me about it and explain its true nature
first, and then, if you have done so satisfactorily,
I will set you free.' 'Very well,' said the 'Efrit,
and spoke as follows:

" 'Know, O damsel, that there lived near the
city of El Maras a certain merchant who pos-
sessed wealth and cattle and had a wife and
children, and God had also endowed him with
the knowledge of the languages of beasts and
birds. The abode of this merchant was in the
country, and he had in his stable an ass and a
bull. Now the bull envied the ass excessively,
because the stall of the ass was much larger
and far more luxuriously appointed than his
own, and the bull, being proud, considered it
unseemly for himself to sleep in such mean
surroundings while the ass enjoyed each night
the comforts of a king. Therefore, the bull began sleeping in the ass's stall, taking up the
lion's share of the space and using as his bed
all of the straw which the stable slave spread
daily upon the floor.

" 'Upon finding out about the conduct of the

bull, the merchant was excessively angered, and ordered the stable slave to extend by five cubits the length of the wall which divided the two stalls and which measured four cubits, so that the bull, whose tether measured only nine cubits, could not pass around it. The stable slave did as he was bidden and made the wall five cubits longer, but the next morning he came running to the merchant and cried, "Master, last night the bull leaped over the top of the wall and slept in the ass's stall as before, for there is an impression of a heavy body in the straw and it is inconceivable that the bull could have walked around the wall when his tether is only nine cubits long." Upon hearing this, the merchant reprimanded the slave for being untruthful, and said, "The wall that separates the two stalls is four cubits high and the bull could not have accomplished such a leap." The stable slave implored him to come to the stable to see for himself, and the merchant, perceiving the slave's agitation, agreed to do so; and lo, just as the stable slave had said, there in the straw of the ass's stall was a deep impression which only an excessively heavy beast such as the bull could have made.

" 'Upon observing this, the merchant himself was agitated, and said within himself, "God has endowed me with the power to understand the languages of beasts and birds, and I have

taken it upon myself to divulge my ability to
no one, neither animal nor man, believing it to
be too sacred to be made known. Therefore I
should not divulge it now by asking this bull
how he accomplished such a marvelous feat."
So instead of asking the bull for an explanation,
the merchant, determined to protect the rights
and privacy of the ass, ordered the stable slave
to heighten the wall between the stalls by six
cubits, so that even were the bull capable of
making so tremendous a leap, the length of his
tether would thwart him. The stable slave did
as he was bidden and heightened the wall by
six cubits, but the next morning he came running to the merchant, so excessively agitated
that he could barely speak, and cried, "Master!
Master! Last night the bull leaped over the wall
and slept beside the ass again, for there is an
impression of a heavy body in the straw!" The
merchant, having heard these words, hurried
to the stable and saw that the stable slave had
again spoken the truth, and the merchant knew
then that he could no longer hide his acquain-
tanceship with the languages of beasts and birds,
and, dismissing the stable slave, proceeded at
once to the stall of the bull.

" 'He addressed himself to the animal as
follows: "Know, O wretched creature, that God
endowed me with the knowledge of the languages of beasts and birds, and know also that

it is in His name that this question is asked:
By what means were you able to leap over a
wall ten cubits in height when your tether measures but nine?" Whereupon the bull, awed by
his master's familiarity with the languages of
beasts and birds, and trembling in his presence,
answered, "Master, there are four ways, not
three, to reach the other side of a wall: by
passing around it, by passing in under it, by
passing over it and *by passing through it.* Know
then, that since I could neither pass around
this wall, nor under it, nor over it, I chose the
fourth way and passed through it."

" 'Upon hearing these words, the merchant
was excessively furious, and it was as though
his resurrection took place. "Why do you lie to
me, O wretched animal?" he cried. "You know
as well as I that that which you claim to have
accomplished can be accomplished only by
Jinn!" "No, master," said the bull, "it can be
accomplished by anyone who knows the secret,
and the secret is this: the wall must be passed
through sideways," whereupon the bull advanced to the wall, turned a little to his left
and passed obliquely through the wall. He then
passed back through it in a similar fashion and
returned to his own stall. The merchant, excessively impressed and believing at last that the
animal had told the truth, cried, "That which
you have accomplished is marvelous indeed;

therefore it is not fitting that a gifted creature such as you should live in quarters less noble than those of a mere ass!" And the merchant called the stable slave and directed him to make the bull's stall larger by two times than that of the ass, and to spread upon its floor each day large quantities of fresh straw. And the bull was pleased, and thereafter he slept in his own stall.

" 'And now, O damsel,' said the 'Efrit, 'it remains but for you to make the following likenesses to understand the true nature of the Veil: The stall of the ass is the land of the Jinn and the stall of the bull is the land of Men, and the wall separating the two stalls is the Veil.' And then the 'Efrit said, 'Since I have fulfilled my part of our covenant, you must now fulfill your part. Liberate me from this bottle, and I vow that I will do you no harm.'

"Before I opened the bottle I first made the 'Efrit swear by the Most Great Name of God that it would be a good Jinni. Then I extracted the stopper, and smoke ascended until it had all come forth, and then it collected together and became as before an 'Efrit of hideous form. It picked up the bottle and turned and went its way and I knew that it would never return. I then had this ring made after the seal of Suleyman Ibn-Da'ud, which was on the stopper, so that were I someday to pass through the Veil into the land of the Jinn they would not dare harm me. But I did not know where the Veil was, and never did I dream that it was close to the palace of the Sultan. I am glad we went through it, Bill, because now I will have a chance to teach the Jinn a lesson with my ring."

IV

John D. Rockefeller and the Thirty-nine Thieves

For a long while Billings didn't say anything. He just sat there on the grass looking at Dunyzad.

Try as he would, he couldn't find the faintest hint of deceit in her violet eyes.

Actually he was more confounded by her description of the 'Efrit than by what the 'Efrit, presumably, had told her about the Veil. The mere thought of a creature being so tall its head was in the clouds boggled his mind.

Hyperbole, of course. She hadn't meant for him to take the description literally.

He had read enough of The Thousand and One Nights to know that many of the stories were full of such nonsense. To her, however, it wasn't nonsense, and whether she had seen the 'Efrit or not and listened to its story, she believed she had. The expression on her face said so.

Well anyway, she had come up with a pretty good description of a space-time warp. But if that was what the Veil really was, he still didn't know whether in passing through it they had jumped ahead in time or had emerged on an alien planet.

"Dunny, have you ever met anyone who has gone through the Veil and come back again?"

"No. But I have heard stories of people who have. That is how I knew at once where we are."

"The . . . ah . . . Jinn. They must pass through it all the time."

"Since the time of our lord Suleyman, most no longer dare, for our lord Suleyman imprisoned all the bad ones in bottles of brass and threw the bottles into the Sea of El-Karkar. Before he did so, there was a Great Battle, of which you may have heard, Bill. Suleyman, enraged at the presence of so many Jinn in the land of Men, prepared his forces, which consisted of men and birds and reptiles, and went forth upon his carpet, with his army following below, and attacked his foes. The Jinn, trembling with terror, tried to flee from him, but he overtook them, and they knelt before him, begging him to spare them. These were the heretical Jinn. But our lord Suleyman, still enraged, sent for brass bottles in which to imprison them, and only those who swore to embrace the faith were allowed to pass back through the Veil to their own land."

Again he looked into her eyes, and again he could find no sign of deceit. But damn it!—the Historical Research Team had told him nothing about such a battle! But neither had they told him anything about the Jinn or the Veil, and he knew there were Jinn because he had seen one, and he knew there was a Veil because he had passed through it, and he knew that since these things were true, the legendary account Dunyzad had given him of the battle must be at least partially based on fact.

And he knew something else: He was never going to get back to Earth-present, wherever or whenever Earth-present was, by sitting under a palm tree listening to her talk. Getting to his feet, he walked over to the time sled, got the screwdriver back out of the toolbox and went to work on the cable. Dunyzad, who had followed him, asked, "What are you going to do, Bill?"

"I'm going to see if we can get back through the Veil."

"But we just got here!"

"I know we did, Dunny. But I don't think it will be sensible for us to stay."

The cable consisted of fourteen different colored strands intricately woven together. If he remembered right, the three he had reconnected were red, black and green. Quickly he disconnected them. "Come on, Dunny," he said, seating himself behind the control board, "we'll give it a whirl."

Reluctantly she boarded the sled and sat down beside him. He showed her how to fasten her seat belt and fastened his own, then he lifted the sled and headed for the oasis they had emerged above. The sun had climbed much higher into the sky, but its rays as yet were only mildly warm upon his back. When they neared the oasis he activated the scrambler and punched out P R on the trans-era keyboard. Well here goes, he thought.

The sled flew over the oasis and the scene remained unchanged.

"Dunny," he said, "does the Veil always stay in the same place?"

"I do not know. We did not go through it, did we."

"I'll bet I disconnected one of the wrong strands."

He deactivated the scrambler, flew back over the oasis and brought the sled down to the ground. He was certain now that it had been a brown strand instead of a green one. Quickly he made the correction, lifted the sled and headed back toward the oasis. Reactivating the scrambler, he punched out P R again. Again the sled flew over the oasis and again the scene remained unchanged.

Maybe he had been wrong about the red

strand. Maybe it had been orange instead of red. He made the correction and tried again.

And got nowhere.

The black strand! It must have been blue, not black!

He tried once more, with the same result.

He began trying completely different combinations. Yellow, tan, orange. White, purple, brown. Red, white, blue. Green, orange, yellow. To no avail. At length Dunyzad said, "I am hungry, Bill."

He saw that the sun was directly overhead. "All right, we'll have something to eat." He brought the sled down on the apron of the oasis and opened two more boxes of rations. Dunyzad had watched him open the mini-cans that morning, and this time she opened hers herself. Her face fell when she found that neither contained cheese. One contained beans and the other miniature wieners. There were plastic spoons to eat the beans with and plastic forks with which to spear the wieners, and in addition to the main course each box contained a candy bar. "Never have I tasted *faludhaj* like this!" she cried after she bit into hers. "Such a marvelous cook you must have, Bill!"

That afternoon he began writing down the various color combinations as he tried them so that he wouldn't use the same combination twice. As the hours went by he realized how much time it might take to find the correct strands. Undaunted, he kept on trying . . . and the sled kept right on flying over the oasis.

It grew hot, and he took his melwatah off and rolled it up and stuffed it into the equipment and ration box. He tried black, green and white.

"Although I do not understand what you are doing, Bill," Dunyzad said when the sun was low in the western sky, "it is rapidly becoming apparent to me that it is not going to get us back through the Veil."

Billings said nothing and tried orange, green and white.

Again, nothing changed.

He was no longer landing between tries but was working with the sled on hover. He reconnected the orange strand and was about to try his luck with a blue one when he saw that there was a dark cloud sweeping over the desert from the east. He turned and stared at it.

Dunyzad had seen it too. "I think it is a rukh, Bill!" she cried. "We must flee!"

It looked like a rain cloud to him, and then he saw that it had wings and legs. He zoomed the sled down to the eastern edge of the oasis and parked it under one of the trees. As he and Dunyzad stared, the rukh made a shallow dive toward one of the other oases, skimmed its treetops, snatched two talonfuls of fruit and then soared back into the sky.

He saw that there were other "clouds." They,

too, began making shallow dives and snatching
fruit. The rise and fall of their wings shook the
treetops and made ripples in the sand. After
gobbling down the fruit in the sky, the rukhs
dived for seconds, then thirds. At long last
they filled their talons and winged off toward
the mountains.

The dinner hour was over.

"Dunny," Billings said in an awed voice,
"there's no such thing as rukhs."

"I did not believe so either, Bill. It is said by
the poets that they live in the mountains of
Kaf. I know now that this must be true."

"I know something else," Billings said. "These
oases aren't real oases. They're orchards. And
whoever planted them planted them for the
rukhs."

"It must have been the Jinn."

He didn't argue. There wasn't enough wind
left in his sails. And besides, she was probably
right.

By this time the sun had set, and he decided
to wait till morning before resuming his attempts to pass through the Veil. He unfastened
his safety belt and got off the sled. "Come on,
Dunny, we're going to camp out for the night."

"Camp out?"

"Yes. I'll put up a tent and we'll sleep in it
beneath the stars."

She unfastened her belt and jumped off the
sled and clapped her hands. "Just like the Bed-

ouins, Bill! Just like the Bedouins! Wait till I
tell my sister Sheherazade! She will be thrilled!
Can I help you put the tent up, Bill?"

"Sure. Come on, we'll put it up now."

It was a pup-size tent with inflatable walls. She
helped him spread it out on the ground and
then he inserted a pneumo-cartridge into the
valve, and there before her wondering eyes the
tent took shape in the twilight. He anchored it
with pegs in case a wind should come up, then
he got a small battery-fed campfire out of the
equipment and ration box, set it in front of the
tent door and turned it on. "A magic fire, Bill!
A magic fire!"

"Don't get too close to it. It gets pretty hot."

Returning to the sled, he got a coffeepot, a
can of coffee and a small metal tripod. After
positioning the tripod over the flames he turned
the campfire to low; then he went to the nearest spring and filled the pot half full. Returning
to the campfire, he put two scoops of coffee
into the filter, put the top on and hung the pot
over the flames on the tripod. Dunyzad, who
had been watching him with fascinated eyes,
gasped when the coffee began to perk.

There were only enough rations in the sled
to sustain one person for ten days, which meant
that he and Dunyzad only had food enough for
five. But this didn't worry him, for they should
be long gone by then. Since there were only

two varieties, he chose corned beef-and-cheese again. He also got two plastic cups, two plastic spoons and a jar of coffee creamer out of the equipment and ration box.

When the coffee was done he poured two cupfuls. He put a spoonful of creamer into Dunyzad's, stirred it in for her and handed her the cup. He always drank his coffee black. When she raised hers to her lips and tasted it, she made a face. He knew what was wrong and got a package of sugar from the sled and put two spoonfuls into her cup. On second thought, he added a third. "Stir it up, Dunny." She did so, and when she tasted the coffee again, she beamed.

Night had fallen by the time they finished eating. He saw that the sky above the mountains had acquired a silvery cast. "Look, Bill," Dunyzad said, "the moon is coming up."

They sat side by side and watched it rise. It was full, just as it had been "last night" when it had risen above the Sultan's palace. But there were two things wrong with it: it was too big, and the man in the moon was gone.

"It is not the same moon," Dunyzad said.

"Yes it is. It's closer, is all, and its face has changed."

"But why should it be closer, and why should its face have changed?"

"Because we're in the future, Dunny."

She was silent for some time. Then she said,

"You mean that the Veil is a doorway to tomorrow?"

"A doorway to a tomorrow thousands of years ahead of yesterday."

"No one ever knew this before, Bill. But it is impossible for me to understand why the passage of time would make the moon change. Or to understand how the future can possibly encircle the Earth."

He remembered that according to legend the mountains of Kaf ringed the Earth, and he wondered uncomfortably if this might not be at least partially true. At the moment he was in no position to say that it wasn't.

"The sky is not the same either," Dunyzad said.

He looked up at the stars. He couldn't see many because of the brightness of the moon. He failed to find a single familiar constellation.

How many years? he wondered. How many centuries? How many millennia?

One thing for sure, he had gotten poor Dunyzad into a fine mess. VIPPnapping her by mistake from in under the Sultan's nose, and then transporting her, however unintentionally, into a future so remote it was as far beyond his grasp as it was beyond hers. And there she sat beside him, not in the least bit worried about their predicament, believing that he was an emir with a palace at least as big as the Sultan's and that he had stolen her away with the no-tion of making her his bride if they should fall in love.

He felt ashamed of himself.

Maybe after they got back through the Veil he would take her to the twenty-first century and maybe he would not. At the moment, his job didn't seem very important to him.

So far, the Veil had thwarted him, but he was certain it couldn't go on thwarting him for very long. And there was another angle he hadn't explored yet: the pumping stations. If they were manned by human beings, they must know about the Veil and ought to be able to tell him how to pass back through. From where he sat he could see the station across the lake. It was a pale blur in the moonlight. The fact that it had no lights didn't discourage him, for there might not be any windows.

He would visit it tomorrow. Meanwhile he would get some sleep. He was tired, and he knew that Dunyzad must be too. But they would not be able to sleep the whole night through. He would have to stand guard part of the time and she would have to stand guard the other part. Not because of the rukhs, for he was certain they did not fly at night, and not merely because the Jinni might be back, but because they were in a strange land which she knew next to nothing about and which he knew nothing about whatsoever.

He would let her sleep first. "Dunny," he said, "I think it's time you went to bed."

"But I do not think I will be able to fall asleep, Bill."

"I don't see why not. You were up all last night."

"That is why. I am up all night almost every night, listening to my sister tell the Sultan stories, and I am used to sleeping days."

"I'll tell you what then. Each of us is going to have to stand guard half the night, so I'll let you stand guard the first half, and by then maybe you'll be sleepy." He crawled into the tent. He hadn't worn a watch, but even if he had, he doubted if she would have been able to tell time by it. Anyway, there was a big watch in the sky. "When the moon is overhead, Dunny, wake me up."

"Where shall I stand, Bill?"

"You don't have to *stand*. Just sit in the doorway. If you see something move in the darkness or hear something besides the chirping of the insects, wake me up. It's getting colder, but the campfire should keep you warm."

She sat down in the doorway, drew up her bloomered legs and wrapped her arms around them. The subdued flames lent her face a roseate cast. When she grew up she was going to be a pretty girl. She was, in fact, a pretty girl now. "I know what I am going to do, Bill," she said. "I am going to tell you one of my sister's stories."

He felt sure it would put him to sleep. "Go ahead."

"I will tell you the first story she told the Sultan." She grew thoughtful. "I know she must be worried about me. And the Sultan—he must be worried about me too."

"I'll get you back to them all right, Dunny."

"I thought you were taking me to your palace."

"Oh. Yes. I am. I mean I'll take you to visit them."

"That will not be necessary, because the first thing I shall do when we reach your palace is to write them and tell them I am all right. But even though they are worried, Bill, I am not in a hurry to leave the land of the Jinn. The Jinn know we are here, because the 'Efrit we saw was a spy, but I am not in the least afraid of them." She held up her left hand and the ring on her middle finger glowed in the firelight. "When they see the seal of Suleyman Ibn-Da'ud they will get down on their knees and beg me not to imprison them in brass bottles and throw them into the sea."

"The story, Dunny—you were going to tell me a story."

"Yes. It is the 'Story of the Merchant and the Jinni.' "

It was as though he were the Sultan and she were Sheherazade. "There was once a certain merchant who had great wealth, and traded extensively with surrounding countries, and one day he mounted his horse and journeyed to a neighboring country to collect what was due to him, and, the heat oppressing him, he sat under a tree in a garden, and put his hand into his saddlebag, and ate a morsel of bread and a date which were among his provisions. Having eaten the date, he threw aside the stone, and immediately there appeared before him an 'Efrit of enormous height, who, holding a drawn sword in his hand, approached him and said, 'Rise, that I may kill thee, as you have killed my son.' The merchant asked him, 'How have I killed your son?' He answered, 'When you ate the date and threw aside the stone, it struck my son upon the chest, and, as fate had decreed against him, he instantly died.'

"The merchant, on hearing these words, exclaimed, 'Verily to God we belong and verily to Him we must return! There is no strength nor power but in God, the High, the Great! If I killed him, I did not do so intentionally, but without knowing it, and I trust in you that you will pardon me.' The 'Efrit answered, 'Your death is indispensable, for you have killed my son.' And so saying, he dragged him and threw him on the ground and raised his arm to strike him with the sword. . . ."

A long while after Billings fell asleep, subconsciously inspired perhaps by the tale Dunyzad had been telling him, he dreamed his way into another Arabian "Night". The dream began innocently enough: he was in his back yard planting early tomatoes. In real life he planted early tomatoes every year so that he could laugh when he drove by the fruit stands where the farmers were charging a dollar apiece for them. The girl he used to go with drove into his yard in her new Fiace-Habley, got out and walked around his mobile home to see what he was doing. She was tall and blonde, and wore tailored slate-blue slacks that made her look like a mailwoman. She taught school. "I should think," she said, "that an intelligent young man such as yourself could find better ways to spend his time than planting tomatoes." "You say that," Billings said, looking up at her from where he was kneeling in the freshly spaded earth, "because you have never fully appreciated the nonpareil taste of an early tomato and have never because of your high income minded the fabulous price demanded for them at the fruit stands." "Basically you have always been a dimwit," the girl, who had never really liked him and whose name was June, said. "Doing something with your hands on a small scale which machines can do ten times better on a large one, just so you can save a few pennies!" "People in your wage bracket," Billings said, "look down their nose at pennies and do not realize that when they are saved every day they multiply themselves at an exponential rate." "I teach mathematics," June said, "and I know that far from multiplying themselves exponentially, pennies do not multiply themselves at all." "You think that way," Billings said, "because you have never read about John D. Rockefeller. He built an empire by saving pennies, and he used to give whole dimes away to the common populace." "I know all about John D. Rockefeller," June said. "I studied about him in college. He was a thief—that was how he got all his money. He used to hide his loot in financial caves. He had thirty-nine thieves working for him, and one time when he and they came with a load of money to their main cave an FBI agent named 'Ali Baba spotted them and hid in a nearby tree. He heard John D. say, 'Open sesame,' to the cave door and saw the cave door open. After the thieves deposited their money they came back out, and John D. said, 'Shut sesame,' to the door, and the door closed, and then the forty thieves rode away. At once 'Ali Baba went to the cave door and said 'Open sesame,' and when the door opened he went inside and stole a bag of thousand-dollar bills. When he came back out he said, 'Shut sesame,' and the door closed, and then he rode home with all his money. His brother, who was named Kasim and who was an IRS agent, found out from 'Ali Baba about the cave and the magic phrases, and early the next morning when 'Ali Baba was still asleep he drove to the cave in a U-Haul truck. After he said, 'Open sesame,' he entered the cave, and the door closed itself behind him. He was so excited about all the money that would soon be his that he couldn't remember the second phrase and was unable to get back out. When the forty thieves returned with another big batch of money they found him there, and they cut him into quarters and hung the quarters just within the cave door to scare other IRS agents away. Then they rode off to steal more money. There was an opening in the roof of the cave, and when a wind sprang up later in the day it made a humming sound as it blew over the hole. *Hum-hum-hum*, it went, but of course poor Kasim could not hear it. *Hum-hum-hum . . .*"

When Billings awoke he could still hear the wind, and he thought that this was odd because there was no wind to hear. He saw that it was broad daylight. Dunyzad was still sitting in the tent doorway, her arms still locked around her legs. Her head was resting on her knees and she was sound asleep.

He should have known better than to have put a fifteen-year-old girl on guard. But everything seemed to be fine, so no harm had been done. He sat up. "Dunny, it's morning," he said.

She looked at him sleepily as he crawled out of the tent. He stood up and stretched his arms. He had had a good night's sleep and felt like a

million dollars. But all was not quite right after
all. There was a strange acrid smell in the air,
and that darned humming sound would not go
away. Presently he saw why. Moving slowly
around the oasis were whirling pillars of sand
just like the one Dunyzad and he had seen
yesterday and which had transformed itself into
a Jinni. *Hum-hum-hum*, they went. *Hum-hum-
hum*.

V

The Mother Bird

"Stand back, Bill!" Dunyzad cried. "I will drive them away!"

She had jumped to her feet and was standing beside him, ready to bring her ring into action. There was no way to tell how many pillars there were, but it was evident that they had the oasis surrounded. He drew his icer.

Dunyzad's chin was thrust out and her truculent expression would have been comical under less potentially dangerous circumstances. He pulled her back into the trees. "Dunny, there's a whole army of them!"

She was mad. "I do not care how many there are! I am not afraid of them!" Then, "Look, one of them is transmuting!"

The pillar toward which she was pointing had whirled out of line and moved to the edge of the grassy apron. Grapnellike hands appeared, big splayed feet; a kettlelike head. It looked exactly like the Jinni Dunyzad and he had seen yesterday, except that it was bigger. It regarded the two human beings with its fanwheellike eyes. It ground its tombstonelike teeth. Then it turned back into a pillar and rejoined the troops. It left an acrid smell behind it.

"I think they're merely curious about us," Billings said. "I don't think they mean us any harm."

"Ha!"

"You've got a chip on your shoulder."

She glanced at her left shoulder and then at her right. "There is nothing on my shoulders. But that is not what you meant, is it, Bill."

"I meant that you're looking for trouble."

"It is they who are looking for trouble."

"I don't think so—see, they're going away."

The pillars had stopped circling the oasis and were heading toward the lake. He counted them as they whirled across the water. There were only twenty; he had thought there were more than that. At length one of the oases hid the last of them from view.

"They are returning to the mountains," Dunyzad said. "I think their city must be there."

"How do you know they live in a city?"

"I do not know, but I have heard that the Jinn do. It is called the City of Brass. Come on,

Bill—we will follow them on your magic carpet and find out."

"Dunny, we aren't going to follow anybody. We're going to try to get back through the Veil." Billings pointed to the dome across the lake. "First, though, we're going to visit that pumping station and see if anyone is inside."

"Pumping station?"

"I think that it and all the other domes are places that pump water."

"Where?"

"To the ocean."

"From the lake?"

"Yes. I think that the lake is a reservoir and that the water is pumped underground to them."

"But maybe the water flows underground."

He had to admit that this was a possibility, for the lake was on slightly higher ground.

"I think it is a fort with Jinn in it," Dunyzad said.

"We'll go see. I don't think the rukhs will bother us because we didn't see any yesterday till almost sunset. We'll have breakfast first, and then we'll break camp."

They washed up in one of the springs and he let Dunyzad borrow his comb. After she combed her hair, he combed his, then he made fresh coffee and opened two more boxes of corned beef and cheese. Dunyzad put four spoonfuls of sugar into her coffee. When she finished her corned beef and cheese she looked into her ration box, hopeful of finding a candy bar. He got one for her out of one of the wieners-and-beans boxes.

After he deflated the tent, she folded it up, and he returned it to the equipment and ration box. He washed the coffeepot in the spring and returned it to the box too, along with the jar of creamer, the package of sugar, the can of coffee and the deactivated campfire. He kicked the empty ration cans and the plastic cups and spoons under a bush. He had only been in the land of the Jinn for a day and a night, and already he was littering.

"Let's go, Dunny."

They fastened their seat belts and he lifted the sled. After all the futile flying around they had done yesterday, air travel should have become old hat to her, but at once her face became radiant. Her whole body seemed to glow, and her black hair danced in the wind of their passage. He remembered the girl he used to go with, the one he had dreamed about last night. Compared to Dunyzad, she was like a stick of wood.

As they flew over the lake he looked down into the water. It was so clear he could see all the way to the bottom. He glimpsed a number of fish, and wished he had his fishing rod and reel.

The dome was about half a mile inland. It

proved to be smaller than he had expected and he was struck by the smoothness of its surface. Not only were there no windows, he could see no sign of a door either. Perhaps there was one on the other side.

As he and Dunyzad grew closer, he saw that the structure was ovoid and could not truly be classified as a dome. Its sides did not rise in a straight line from the ground; instead, they were as rounded as the roof. Dunyzad gasped. "Bill!" she cried. "It is an egg!"

"You mean that it's shaped like an egg."

"No, I mean it is an egg! A rukh's egg!"

"Even a rukh," Billings said, "couldn't lay an egg that big."

He flew down for a closer look. As he did so, he saw a vast shadow sweeping toward them across the desert from the direction of the mountains. Raising his eyes, he saw that a huge superjet was coming in for a landing. "It is the mother bird!" Dunyzad screamed. "Fly away, Bill! Fly away!"

The superjet was dark-brown in color and its landing gear had feet instead of wheels. Its prow was accipitrine and had been painted a dirty yellow. There were two pilot windows. They were golden and had black dots in their centers. The wings extended in both directions all the way to the horizon.

Or at least they seemed to.

Billings now knew how a seagull must feel

when a real superjet was zooming toward it.
But he wasn't a seagull. He was a thinking
human being on board a sled that could travel
in time. On the trans-era keyboard there was a
fifteen-minute time-jump key whose purpose
was to extricate a time traveler from dire
difficulties. He found it with his forefinger and
jammed it down. Nothing happened. Naturally
not. How could the sled possibly jump ahead
in time when the damned cable was partially
disconnected? He groaned. The scaled fingers
of one of the bird's enormous feet closed around
the sled and the rukh soared into the sky.

Well here I am, Billings thought, as the tiny
green dots of the oases began drifting past far
below, being borne away with a ninth-century
Arabian teenager by a bird so big it thinks boa
constrictors are worms!

He was dreaming of course. Any moment
now he would wake up in his mobile home. He
would get up, put coffee on to perk and look
out through the kitchen window at the junkyard
that adjoined his lot and rejoice in the sight of
all the dilapidated cars.

But the dream continued, and finally he forced
himself to accept it as fact. His turban had
fallen off, and Dunyzad's arms were locked
around his neck and she was even more scared
than he was. But the time sled was still upright

and hadn't been damaged, and he still had his icer in his pocket.

Things could have been worse.

Only two of the rukh's fingers were locked around the sled. He fixed the beam of the icer on the nearest one, and held it there. Then he sat back grimly to wait till the finger's numbness caused the rukh to loosen its grip.

It was flying in a southeasterly direction; the down-draft from its wings buffeted the sled at rhythmic intervals and its huge foot blocked his view of the sky. Dunyzad removed her arms from around his neck, but he saw that she was still scared. "Hey, Dunny—don't worry. We'll get away. See, I'm freezing its foot."

She achieved a smile. "Is—is that what that little tube does?"

"It generates a beam of subzero energy that diffuses itself in the target's flesh." He was speaking half in English and half in Arabic, and he knew she didn't know what he was talking about, but perhaps the words themselves would reassure her whether she knew their meaning or not. "Pretty soon the rukh'll drop us, and when it does it may not even notice we're gone."

"It had better drop us pretty soon because we are almost to the mountains. When it reaches its perch it will probably eat us."

When he looked down he saw that they were already over the mountains. Although the mountains were little more than oversized hills, some of their peaks jutted up like ragged pillars, and the rukh was flying so low the sled almost collided with one of them. Other rukhs were perched on some of the peaks. Watching their eggs with their telescopic eyes. The desert, among other things, was a vast incubator.

The sled gave a slight lurch. The rukh's grip was loosening. "Hang on, Dunny—in a minute we'll be free."

He saw the nest below them then, with all the baby rukhs in it. They were as big as houses and all of them had their mouths open. The nest, with its maze of broken and interwoven trees, made him think of the forest that the Tunguska meteorite had leveled. "They—they must bring their young here after the eggs have hatched," Dunyzad said in an awed voice. Then she threw her arms around his neck and kissed him. "Oh, Bill, we are done for! Now we will never know whether we would have fallen in love!"

He had wasted his time trying to freeze the rukh's finger, for the rukh let go of the sled of its own accord. However, the sled did not fall, for the intra-era inertia regulator was still on, and he and Dunyzad sailed over the cavernous mouths of the baby rukhs. Quickly he nosed the craft upward so it would not slam into the next mountain. He then gave the regulator all the juice he coud get from the batteries and zoomed the sled over a gargoylelike peak. To the north he saw a vast, green valley.

The rukh's flyby took it at least two miles beyond the nest. No doubt it thought Billings and Dunyzad had become birdseed by this time, and it did not learn otherwise till it began the return journey. The shrill scream it emitted when it saw the sled aroused the other rukhs, and they took off from their peaks on long glides, winged higher into the sky and joined the first rukh in the chase. Billings headed toward the valley.

Dunyzad had removed her arms from around his neck and was looking to the rear. "One of them is just behind us, Bill!"

He did not need to be told; he could hear the awesome flapping of the great wings. The valley seemed hopelessly far away. He could see clusters of trees and green fields. In the far distance he could see what appeared to be a city. If he could reach one of the clusters of trees it would provide them with sanctuary from the rukhs, but he knew he could not reach the nearest one in time. Over his shoulder he glimpsed one of their pursuer's feet. The fingers were spread wide, ready to grab the sled. He tried to get more juice out of the batteries. He could not. This time, he and Dunyzad were really done for. He didn't care insofar as he himself was concerned. In a way he deserved to die. VIPPnapping the wrong girl and lying to her and inadvertently taking her into the remote future had been bad enough without sealing her fate by mistaking a rukh's egg for a pumping station. Yes, he deserved to die.

"A cave!" Dunyzad cried. "Look, Bill—look! A cave! There, on the mountainside!"

It was hardly a stone's throw away and the mouth was more than wide enough to admit the time sled. He veered the craft so sharply that had it not been for their belts he and Dunyzad would have been thrown from their seats. The rukh that was on their tail tried to veer too, but couldn't do so in time. Billings didn't decelerate till the last moment; then, deftly, he guided the sled into the cave.

VI

Fort Knox

"I smell horses," Dunyzad said.

Billings did too, but there was enough light coming through the cave's mouth to show that there were no horses to smell.

Still shaken from their flight from the rukhs, he deactivated the regulator and got a flashlight out of the equipment and ration box. Flicking the light on, he unfastened his belt, stepped off the sled and moved the beam back and forth over the granite floor. He found what he had expected to find: traces of dried-up manure.

Dunyzad had also gotten off the sled. "Since wild horses do not live in caves," she said, "the ones that were here must have been ridden here."

"From the other side of the Veil?"

"Perhaps. But maybe there are horses in the

land of the Jinn. Shine your magic light around
some more, Bill. Maybe whoever was here left
something behind."

He did so, but all he found was more manure.
He played the light over the rest of the granite
chamber. It proved to be far larger than he had
thought. The highest point of the concave ceiling was at least fifteen feet above the floor. The
walls were relatively smooth and the floor was
devoid of fallen rock. Probably it had been
cleared away by whoever had turned the place
into a stable. He saw that the chamber did not
take up the entire cave. Opposite the mouth
there was a tunnel which led deeper into the
mountain.

He wondered if anyone or anything lived
back there. He hoped not.

Dunyzad went over to the cave's mouth and
looked out. "Bill, they left a trail."

He turned off the flashlight and joined her.
The trail led diagonally down the mountainside in a westerly direction. Certain that the
rukhs had given up the chase, he leaned through
the mouth for a better look. The churned up
hoofprints told him that the horsemen (he assumed they must be men since it was difficult
to picture a Jinni upon a horse) must have been
here many times. It also opened wide the possibility that they would be back.

Dunyzad had raised her eyes from the trail

and was looking down into the valley. "I think that is where the Jinn live, Bill."

Whether or not they did, it was clear that someone did, for the evenly laid out fields as well as the distant city indicated that the valley was inhabited. A stream threaded the greenness, and even finer threads ran out from it between the fields. Irrigation ditches. And the clusters of trees—they were probably orchards.

He wondered if there were binoculars in the equipment and ration box. He rummaged through it and finally found a small pair on the bottom. Removing them from their case, he went back to the cave mouth and focused their lenses on the nearest cluster of trees. Yes, an orchard. The trees looked a little bit like apple trees. Suddenly he gasped, but not because of the trees. There were people picking fruit from their branches!

Dunyzad, who of course had never seen nor heard of binoculars, had nevertheless divined that the strange object in Billings' hands brought faraway objects up closer. "Let me look, Bill! Let me look!"

He handed her the binoculars. "Point them at that nearest cluster of trees. Tell me what you see."

She did so. An instant later she said, "Jinn! I see Jinn!"

"Oh for Pete's sake!" Billings said. "Those are people, not Jinn!"

"I see the people too. They are picking fruit and putting it in boxes. But there are two Jinn standing guard over them so they cannot escape." She handed the binoculars back. "There is a Jinni on each side of the orchard. You look again, Bill, and maybe this time you will see them too."

He did so. Sure enough, she was right. Both Jinn had taken on "human" form and had the attitudes of guards. "All right, I see them," he said. "But just because they happen to be guards doesn't mean the people picking the fruit are prisoners. Maybe they're there to protect the people from the rukhs."

"Ha!"

He saw no point in arguing with her. She had it in for the Jinn, and that was all there was to it.

He focused the binoculars on another orchard. It was farther away, but he discerned several fruit pickers just within its perimeter and he made out two more Jinn. He tried one of the fields. He could not see it clearly enough to tell what was growing on it, but he spotted several tiny shapes moving about in the greenness.

He began surveying the rest of the valley. He traced the stream back as far as distance would permit. It sparkled in the sunlight, and the mere sight of it made him thirsty. Its source must be a mountain lake. He followed its forward path.

The stream wound among the orchards, then entered a small green forest at the feet of the mountains that bordered the valley on the west, and disappeared.

He looked at several more fields but saw no sign of life in them. Presently he found a narrow dirt road with a number of crude carts lined up on it. Otherwise the road was empty.

Finally he focused the binoculars on the city. Distance thwarted him, and all he could distinguish was a high wall and a tall tower. The tower glowed in the sunlight and the absurd thought crossed his mind that it might be made of gold.

Dunyzad was tugging on his arm. "Let me see the city, Bill! Let me see the city!"

He gave her the binoculars. A moment later she gasped. "Bill, it is the City of Brass!"

"How do you know it's the City of Brass if you've never seen the City of Brass?"

"Because of the tower. It is made of brass!"

He had to admit that brass was easier to believe than gold, but he still found the idea preposterous. "Dunny, do you have any idea how difficult it would be to melt and pour that much metal, not to mention making a mold for it?"

She had lowered the binoculars. Her violet eyes were bright with excitement. "The tower would not glow like that if it were not made of brass!"

"It might be painted the color of brass."

"No. It *is* brass!"

"Dunny, you can't tell folklore from fact!"

She looked at him blankly. "What I mean is," he explained, "You've been listening to your sister's stories for so long that you've come to believe they are real."

"I do *not* believe they are real! She has such a wild imagination that anyone who believed what she said would be crazy. And she exaggerates. You would not believe how much she exaggerates! But even if I did believe her stories, Bill, she has never once told the Sultan one about the City of Brass."

Billings vaguely remembered seeing such a story in the microfilm *Arabian Nights' Entertainments* which Historical Research had lent him the night before his departure, but he didn't contradict her. Perhaps she had been absent when Sheherazade had told it to the Sultan, or maybe Sheherazade had yet to tell it. He hadn't read it. Now he wished he had.

"Come on, Dunny—let's take a look at the rest of the cave."

He returned the binoculars to the equipment and ration box. Before they set out he reconnected the green and white strands to the scrambler. Just in case. The tunnel proved to be wide enough for them to walk abreast, but he stayed a few steps ahead of her, his icer in one hand and the flashlight in the other. The tunnel had been widened in places so that the width would remain constant; otherwise it was a natural fissure in the granite. It veered first one way and then another. The floor slanted slightly upward and had been cleared of fallen rock. In several places where dust had sifted down he saw footprints. They were too indistinct for him to tell whether they had been made recently or had been there a long time, but they suggested that the owners of the horses might have had their headquarters deeper in the cave.

At length he discerned daylight up ahead. This failed to reassure him, for a second entrance to the cave would merely add to his and Dunyzad's vulnerability. But instead of leading to a second entrance, the tunnel debouched into a chamber even larger than the one they had left. The source of the daylight was a wide and inaccessible fissure in the ceiling. It brought to mind a skylight, and the sunlight streaming through it illuminated the entire chamber.

When he saw what the chamber contained, he stopped and stared.

So did Dunyzad.

After an awed silence, Billings returned his icer to his trousers pocket and laid the flashlight on the floor. Beside him, Dunyzad whispered, "We are rich, Bill."

Richer, he thought, than either Croesus or John D. Rockefeller had ever dreamed of being.

There were piles of gold ingots. There were piles of silver ingots. There were heaps of jewelry. There were bales of silk. There were rolls of Persian rugs. There were congeries of miscellaneous household items of the kind usually found for sale in ninth-century Arabian bazaars. The chamber was a treasure-trove.

He knew that he was gazing upon loot—loot which the horsemen must have been bringing to the cave for years. And since it was obviously Arabian loot, the horsemen knew how to pass through the Veil.

No doubt they rode across the desert at night when the rukhs were asleep and came through a pass in the mountains to the cave.

He picked up one of the gold ingots. It weighed at least twenty pounds. The last market report he had seen said that gold was selling for $1002.03 an ounce.

Dunyzad had picked up a lamp. It was made of brass and looked like an elongated teakettle. "I have heard that if you rub a lamp shaped like this a good Jinni will appear."

He hardly heard her. He had just bought a house—a Greek Revival mansion with a six-columned portico—and now he was out looking at cars. He purchased two Fiace-Hableys and an antique 1960 Mercedes Benz convertible. While he was in town he bought three $600

suits, ten $75 dress shirts, three $30 ties, five
$15 pairs of socks and four pairs of Gucci shoes.
Then he went to New England and bought a
pied à terre in Maine, after which he dashed
down to Florida and purchased a huge beach
house. A private plane? Yes, of course. He
bought one of the new Cessnas. He would take
flying lessons. He saw a golf course that was
for sale and bought that too. He laid the money
right down. In the trunk of his Fiace-Habley he
carried three big suitcases full of $1,000 bills
so that he would never run short.

"Bill?"

He saw that Dunyzad had returned the lamp
to the pile of articles she had picked it up
from and was looking at him. "Are you all right,
Bill?"

"Sure I'm all right."

"That ingot you are holding must be kind of
heavy."

"I was only hefting it," he said, and replaced
it on the pile. When he did so he came back
down to earth with a great big thump. This
wasn't his treasure and it wasn't Dunyzad's,
even though they had found it. It belonged to
the people and the institutions it had been
stolen from. On the other hand, it would probably never be returned, which meant that de
facto it belonged to the thieves who had stolen
it. Surely it would not be unethical to steal
from a thief.

He put the matter from his mind for the time being and began exploring the rest of the chamber. Ranged along the rear wall were several big earthenware jars, two of which were filled with oil. He saw that niches had been cut into the chamber's walls at regular intervals and that lamps had been placed in them to illuminate the chamber at night. The lamps were simple affairs, not in the least like the one Dunyzad had picked up. In addition to the big jars there was a large number of smaller ones with wide mouths which Dunyzad said were *kullehs*. All were empty and would be ideal for carrying water in. Tonight he would fly down to the stream and fill some of them. He would also fill some of them with fruit, assuming it proved to be edible, for he and Dunyzad would eventually run out of food if he didn't supplement their supply. He would fly back to the desert early tomorrow morning. Hopefully the rukhs would not yet be abroad. If they were, he could easily elude them by time-jumping the sled. He would then resume his attempts to pass through the Veil, but if he had no more luck than he had had yesterday he and Dunyzad might wind up being permanent residents in the land of the Jinn.

Ever since entering the treasure chamber he had been experiencing déjà vu. Finally he realized why. It was almost exactly like the cave he had dreamed about last night—the one in which 'Ali Baba had found the "forty thieves'" treasure. And the treasure he and Dunyzad had found was almost exactly like the treasure in the Sheherazade story.

Pure coincidence, of course.

"I am hungry, Bill," Dunyzad said.

He saw that the sun's rays were coming down vertically through the fissure in the ceiling. "I am too, Dunny. Come on, we'll go back to the carpet." A thought crossed his mind. It had been lurking on the sidelines for a long time. "Dunny, you're supposed to face Mecca and pray five times a day and so far I haven't seen you do so once. "Why?"

"There is no Mecca in the land of the Jinn—that is why. Is that why you do not do so either, Bill?"

He had trapped himself. But since he had already lied himself blue in the face he didn't see what difference one more lie would make. Anyway, all he had to do was nod his head.

Dunyzad had corned beef and cheese and he had wieners and beans. He gave her the candy bar out of his box. He wished he had water to make coffee with. It would have been nice, in fact, if they'd just had some water to drink.

They ate sitting on the edge of the sled. After they finished he got the binoculars and they went over and sat down side by side in the mouth of the cave. They kept passing the binoculars back and forth. The people were still at work in the orchards and, presumably, in the fields, and the Jinn still stood guard.

At length he set the binoculars aside and they discussed the treasure. Dunyzad had come to the same conclusion about its provenance as he had. "It is too bad," she remarked, "that your magic carpet is not bigger. Then we could take all the gold and silver ingots and all the jewels with us."

"Dunny, none of that stuff belongs to us!"

"It does not belong to the thieves either, even though it might just as well, since it will never be returned. So if we steal it we will not really be stealing it since it has already been stolen and we will be taking it from thieves."

Her thoughts had roughly followed his. "Well maybe we can take just a little."

"A little! We should take all the magic carpet will hold!"

"We'll see."

"I can just see the expressions on the thieves' faces when they come back and see that most of their treasure is gone!"

"Let's hope," Billings said, "that they don't come back before *we*'re gone."

The rest of the afternoon seemed to drag, and after a while it occurred to him that the days must have grown longer. He hadn't noticed yesterday because he had been so busy trying to pass through the Veil, and this morning so many things had happened that time had flown by. But simple logic said that if the sun had grown old, so had Earth, and that its axial rotation must have slowed.

He was curious about the city, and became more so as the afternoon dragged by. He wanted to fly over it for a closer look, but of course he didn't dare do so in the daytime. He knew he could accelerate the passage of time by boarding the sled with Dunyzad and jumping the craft ahead, but he was far from impatient enough to do so.

Toward the end of the day the people in tho nearest orchard began loading the boxes of fruit they had picked onto the carts. Presumably the people in the fields and in the other orchards were following a similar operation, although even through the binoculars he could not see any of them clearly enough to tell, nor could he tell, of course, what they had picked. But it was evident that this must be harvest time.

The carts, after they were loaded, began moving in the direction of the city, pulled and pushed by the people who had loaded them. No doubt it was a lengthy procession, but he could only see the tail end of it. The two Jinn transformed themselves into pillars and fell in behind.

He hated to admit it, but Dunyzad was right. The people were prisoners.

The valley was a prison farm.

The city, then, must be a prison.

After he and Dunyzad had supper they sat in the mouth of the cave and watched the moon rise. It seemed no less full than it had been last night. Below them the valley turned into silver. Except for the distant city. It had acquired an odd, bluish cast.

He saw no point in waiting any longer and got up and went back through the tunnel into the treasure chamber and got six kullehs. Dunyzad, who had accompanied him, helped him carry them back. "What are you going to do with them, Bill?"

He set hers and his on the sled. "I'm going to fly down and get some water and maybe pick some fruit."

"You are going to leave me *here*?"

She would be a lot safer with him, he decided, than she would be alone in the cave, even though a certain amount of risk would be involved if he carried out his plan to fly over the city. "No, you can come too."

He was taken unawares when she put her arms around his neck and kissed him before climbing up on the sled. After he replaced the binoculars in the equipment and ration box, he sat down beside her, fastened his belt and saw to it that hers was fastened too. The moonlight coming through the cave's mouth made a silver cameo of her face and he sat there looking at her for some time. He had not yet been able to figure her out. The little bit which Smith, Historical Research's chief adviser, had told him about ninth-century Arabian girls simply didn't jell if you used her as an exemplar. Granted, passing himself off as an emir had worked, and granted, she had posed no objections to being borne away on a "magic carpet." But Smith had also said that ninth-century Arabian girls felt naked without their yashmaks and that they were reticent in the presence of men. Dunyzad was about as reticent as a twenty-first-century junior high school cheerleader and if she had ever worn a yashmak she certainly didn't seem to miss it. And then he remembered that when Historical Research had briefed him, mention had been made that Sheherazade was of Persian descent, which meant of course that Dunyzad was too. But this explained nothing, for he was certain that ninth-century Persian girls didn't act like twenty-first-century junior high school cheerleaders either and that they too probably felt naked without a yashmak.

But Smith hadn't been talking about teenagers, he had been talking about adults. Maybe that was the answer.

Billings didn't think so. He was inclined to think that the real reason Dunyzad acted the way she did was that she was Dunyzad and not part of some dry page out of the past.

She was looking at him now, no doubt wondering why he was just sitting there looking at her. He activated the intra-era regulator, hit the hover button, turned the sled around and guided it out over the valley.

VII
The Ghuleh

He brought the sled down on a wide spiral and landed on the bank of the stream near one of the orchards. The water was argent in the moonlight and its ripples danced and sang.

Dunyzad knelt on the bank the minute she got off the sled and began cupping water into her mouth. He joined her and began cupping it into his; there was no other way to find out whether it was fit to drink. Like the water they had drunk in the oases, it tasted like champagne.

He filled three of the *kullehs* and wedged them between the toolbox and the equipment and ration box. Dunyzad took off her slippers, rolled up the legs of her bloomers and began wading in the stream. "I wish I could take a bath, Bill," she said.

He wished he could too. And then he thought,

Why not? They seemed to have the whole valley to themselves, and morality, both twenty-first-century and ninth, could easily be maintained if he went downstream a short ways. "You go ahead, Dunny. I'm going around that bend and take one too."

The bend was farther downstream than he had thought. After rounding it, he removed his clothes and stepped into the rippling water. It had not seemed cold when he drank it, but it seemed cold now. He waded into the middle of the stream. Even here, the water was only about two feet deep. He lay down in it and gasped; then he let its coolness ripple over his legs and arms and chest. The moonlight fell upon his face like silver rain.

He lay there half floating for a long time. Total relaxation crept through him. He ascribed it to the massaging effect of the water; he did not discover till later that it had a different cause. He felt as though he could lie there forever, and only through an effort of will did he finally force himself to rise. Even then, reality did not quite come back; he donned his clothes and slipped his feet into his slippers as though half in a dream. He saw then that the moonlight had cast a shadow on the stream. He was only mildly surprised when he raised his eyes and saw a woman standing on the opposite bank.

She was holding out her hands to him. Her

black hair, paled by the moonlight, tumbled down past her face and lay in arabesques upon her white shoulders. Although her back was to the moon he could see her face clearly. Compared to it, Dunyzad's was that of a gamine. Wide-apart eyes, large and slightly slanted, arched by bird-wing brows, a Gioconda nose, lips whose redness even the semi-darkness could not dispel. Golden cups concealed her breasts; her belly was bare and a jewel adorned her navel. A white filmy skirt came halfway to her knees, emphasizing the length of her legs and enhancing their flawless curvature.

Her lips moved; he seemed to hear her words. "Come with me to my palace. It is a place of many delights. We will feast on sikbaj and I will fill your cup again and again with wino."

He waded across the stream. When he climbed up on the opposite bank, she took his hand. Her scent engulfed him, made his mind reel. He went with her like a little child. His hair, still soaking wet, clung to his forehead and to the sides of his face, but he was only vaguely aware of it. Presently he saw her palace. He could not understand why he had not seen it before. It rose high into the sky; its windows were like stars, and the moon, mysteriously, had transformed itself into a dome.

They came to a stone wall and she led him through a vaulted entrance into the palace garden. Multitudinous flowers added their scent to hers, and he became truly drunk. In a small clearing a fountain twinkled, and near it stood a stone table at which were seated three beautiful children, a girl and two boys. They wore tuniclike garments made of the same filmy material as the woman's skirt. They smiled up at him. They had long, sharp teeth. "These are my children," the woman said. "Sit down with them and I will get the *sikbaj*, which the cook has just prepared, and the wine."

He sat down between the girl and one of the boys. The other boy sat across the table from him. The woman vanished into the shadows. He marveled at the children's beauty. He could tell from their faces that they were hungry. He was mildly hungry himself. *Sikbaj* would taste good after two days of wieners and beans and corned beef and cheese. If he remembered correctly, it was a dish made of meat, wheat-flour and vinegar.

Presently he heard footsteps behind him, and turning, saw that the woman had reappeared. She was carrying a silver tray which glittered in the moonlight. She gave him a warm smile and its warmth went all through him. Then, out of the corner of his eye, he saw Dunyzad. She had come to the party too! He was about to welcome her when, to his astonishment, she streaked out of the shadows and tackled the woman. The tray went flying, only he saw now that it wasn't a tray. It was a butcher knife.

"Bill!" Dunyzad screamed. "They are ghuls!"

Ghuls? At first he couldn't grasp the meaning of the word. Then he realized that the girl and the boy he was sitting between had seized his arms. Their faces had narrowed and their lips had thinned. Their hair, which had been neatly combed, had become matted and caked with dirt. They wore rags. The girl was about to sink her long, sharp teeth into his arm. He leaped to his feet and jerked both arms free. He kicked the girl away and stepped back. The two boys started toward him, but he had his icer out by this time, and quick-froze them. The girl had climbed up on the table and tried to leap upon him. He froze her in midair.

Dunny! he thought. Dunny! Turning, he saw that the woman had pinned her to the ground and had retrieved the knife. He saw her objectively for the first time. Her hair hung in hanks about her shriveled face. Her body was gaunt, her legs were bony and covered with sores. She, too, wore rags. Billings iced her as she raised the knife, then ran forward and pulled Dunyzad from beneath her. She clung to him. He saw that the palace and the garden had disappeared and that the table had turned into an oblong chunk of granite spattered with stains. He and Dunyzad were standing in a ruin.

Her hair was soaking wet too, and even more of a mess than his was. Without saying anything, he handed her his comb. She took it without a

word and combed her hair. Its wetness caused
it to cling tightly to her head, and her cheeks
seemed fuller, her face almost round. When
she finished, he combed his.

By then, both of them had calmed down. "I
saw her lead you away," she said, reattaching
her barrette, "and I got dressed as fast as I
could and followed. She is a ghuleh, Bill. She
and her children would have eaten you!"

Billings shuddered. He was still not quite up
to saying anything. "I know you did not kill
them," Dunyzad went on, "because it is impossible to kill someone who is already dead. How
long will they remain like that?"

Once again folklore had intruded itself upon
reality, but this time he didn't look down his
nose at it. He qualified it instead. "They can't
really be dead or the icer wouldn't have worked,
so they won't thaw out for a long time. She—
she cast some kind of a spell over me. I thought
she was beautiful. I thought her children were
beautiful too."

"She did not cast it over me because she did
not see me, so when I saw her I knew right
away she was a ghuleh."

"Are ghuls Jinn?"

"I do not know. But they are on the other
side of the Veil too. They live in ruins like this
one ... I do not understand, Bill, why you
have never heard of them before, or why you
know nothing about the Jinn. Are you a poet,

perhaps, as well as an emir, who spends all his time writing verse in a little room high in a tower, pretending the rest of the world does not exist?"

He almost told her the truth then and there, and perhaps he would have if she had waited for his answer. But she didn't. Instead she said, "My bath made me hungry, Bill. Come, we will go and pick some fruit." And so he set the truth aside.

VIII

The City of Brass

After recrossing the stream they made their way to the nearest orchard. As they neared the trees he could smell their fruit. The smell made him think of cantaloupes, but he knew that cantaloupes didn't grow on trees.

The orchard was the same one he had first looked at through the binoculars, but seen up close the trees didn't remotely resemble apple trees. They were much too big, and even in the moonlight he could see that their leaves were palmate.

The lowest branches proved to be at least ten feet from the ground. There were clusters of fruit hanging on some of them, but most of them were bare. The fruit pickers must have used ladders, but if they had, they had hidden them well. "Come on, Dunny," he said, halting beneath one of the clusters. "Climb up and stand on my shoulders."

She kicked off her slippers, climbed up his back and balanced herself. Her bloomers were wet from wading across the stream, and drops of water ran down his back. "Hurry up and pick some," he said. "I don't need another bath!"

She giggled, and dropped one of the fruits into his hands. It looked like a cantaloupe and it felt like one, so why not call it one? "Can you catch another, Bill?"

"Go ahead."

She dropped one more, then jumped to the ground like a Hollywood stunt girl. Enough moonlight filtered through the interstices in the foliage to provide all the light he needed, and he cut one of the cantaloupes in two. It was filled with pulpy seeds, just like a real cantaloupe would be. He shook them out and cut each half into quarters and tasted the flesh. The flavor transcended that of conventional cantaloupes. Dunyzad had already devoured the flesh of one of the other quarters and had started on a second one. "Bill, let me climb up on your shoulders and pick some more!"

"Let's finish these two first."

It did not take them long; then, balancing herself on his shoulders, she dropped down two more. After he sliced them they ate the flesh, sitting side by side on the ground, the moonlight patterning them with silvery ara-

besques. Billings saw an owl looking down at
them from one of the trees. No doubt this was
the first cantaloupe picnic it had ever viewed.
Dunyzad saw it too. "Did you know, Bill, that
when an owl watches a man and a woman, it
means they may be falling in love?"

"I think it's looking for a mouse," Billings
said.

"No. It is watching us."

"You're not a woman."

"I am almost one."

"I think," Billings said nervously, "that we'd
better get back to the magic carpet."

He had forgotten to bring the kullehs—they
would have been of no use any use anyway,
since they were too small—but there was no
reason why he and Dunyzad couldn't carry some
cantaloupes back to the sled. She climbed up
on his shoulders again and dropped down two
more, then she dropped two more for good
measure onto the ground. Afterward she began
looking for her slippers. Billings joined her in
the search. He had left his flashlight in the
cave and he kept trying to pick up slipperlike
patterns of moonlight. "Why didn't you just
take them off?" he asked. "You didn't have to
kick them into the trees!"

"I did not kick them into the trees!"

"Then where are they?"

"I do not know where they are!"

He tripped over one. She spotted the other a

short distance away. They walked back to the
sled, carrying two cantaloupes apiece, without saying a word. He put the cantaloupes into
the equipment and ration box and Dunyzad
plumped herself down on the seat and fastened
her safety belt. He sat down beside her, fastened his, and lifted the sled into the night sky.
He pointed the prow toward the city.

The fields and the orchards drifted by beneath them. The stream in which they had
bathed wound anfractuously below. He had not
told Dunyzad he was going to fly over the city
and he wondered what her thoughts were as
she sat there staring straight ahead. She was
not about to tell him. "Dunny, I didn't mean to
make you mad."

"I am not mad!"

Not much, she wasn't. He should have left
her in the cave

But if he had, by this time he would have
been devoured by the ghuls.

He felt terrible.

The tower was at this end of the city, compris-
ing part of the wall. It proved to be the source
of the bluish cast he had noticed from the cave.
Deep blue light flowed fanwise from its apex
and bathed the entire city. Apparently there
were no other lights of any kind.

He flew as close to the tower as he dared.
The blue light emanated from a horizontal slot

and should have been no more than a wide
beam; instead, it not only fanned out but became a lake of radiance.

There was only one other aperture. It was on
the side opposite the slot and slightly lower
down, and appeared to be a window. A light so
dim he had not noticed it before showed within
it. In a way, the tower made him think of a
lighthouse, but there was one thing wrong with
the comparison. The surface of the structure
shone softly in the moonlight and he knew he
was looking at metal, and although he could
not tell what kind, he was certain that Dunyzad
was right: the tower was made of brass.

He pictured an enormous ladle hanging from
a sky hook pouring molten metal into a gigantic,
cone-shaped mold, but he knew he was exag-
gerating the difficulties of the operation, that
the tower could have been poured in sections.
It did not look as though it had been, but he
was seeing it in the light of the moon.

"You see, Bill," Dunyzad said, "it *is* the City
of Brass."

"But the *city* isn't brass. Only the tower is."

"The tower must be how it got its name. The
tower is where the Jinn live."

"How do you know that?"

He had flown over the wall, and she pointed
down to the lightless buildings and empty narrow streets that spread out below them on the

bottom of the lake of light. "Do you think they would live there?"

The buildings were boxlike and arranged in square blocks, and one block was exactly like the next. He had noted when passing over the wall that it was constructed of blocks of granite. Probably the buildings were too, although he could not see them clearly enough to tell. But regardless of what they were constructed of, they must be dismal places in which to live. "No, I guess the Jinn wouldn't," he said.

"I think it must be a prison, Bill," Dunyzad said, echoing the thought he had had that afternoon.

But if it was a prison, why was it illuminated with deep-blue rather than ordinary light?

He flew farther out over the buildings and the streets, staying well above the light. The city was not large; by twenty-first-century standards it could not even be called one. In its center there was a big square in the middle of which was what looked like a well. The buildings had a dull monotony about them. Some of the ones along the granite wall looked like warehouses. The carts he had seen on the narrow road were standing in nearby lots. There was only one entrance in the wall. It was wide and vaulted, and the grille of the gate was faintly visible.

He made several passes over the city, looking for some sign of life, but found none. "They must be afraid to come out of their houses at night," Dunyzad said. "I am glad I am up here on the magic carpet with you, Bill."

It dawned on him then that she wasn't the least bit mad at him any more. Usually when a girl got mad at him she sulked for at least a day and sometimes a week. Dunyzad was just a kid, of course, but that didn't cut any ice. He discovered that he liked her now even more than he had before.

Since the city had revealed next to nothing about Earth future he decided to do a little more exploring and guided the time sled through a pass at the valley's end. A vast plateau spread out before them, and he flew out over it, looking down for some sign of life.

The plateau had no business being there, but its presence was easier to accept than that of the mountains. They had appeared and grown old since the time of the Sultan and Sheherazade. The mere thought of the vast amount of time that had gone by chilled him. Since he had discovered that he and Dunyzad were still on Earth he had toyed with the idea that they might be able to go "around" the Veil by traveling back in time. For the first time he realized what a ridiculous idea it was.

There was only one way to make the return trip, and that was by going back the way they had come.

The thought frightened him, because he knew that even if he did find the right wires to disconnect he might not be successful, that an unknown factor might be involved.

Perhaps he had already disconnected the right ones.

Or perhaps the Veil had moved.

Surely there must be humans on Earth besides those imprisoned in the city. If he could find a town or a real city, some of the inhabitants might know about the Veil. If they did, surely they would know how to pass through it. There had to be a rift of some kind, or else the thieves wouldn't have been able to get through, time and time again.

He flew and flew and flew, but he didn't find a city or a town, or even so much as a single dwelling. All he saw were rock outcroppings, dried-out gullies and bleak expanses of stones and sand. He didn't even see any sign of animals, although he knew there must be insectivores at least, that the land couldn't be completely dead.

Dunyzad hadn't asked him what he was looking for; she knew. Her face looked sad in the moonlight. "I think we are all alone, Bill."

"I guess we are, Dunny."

But he didn't give up. A blur of hills began to show in the distance, and he flew toward them. They edged higher and higher into the sky, but when he reached them he saw that they were as bleak as the plateau. Beyond them the land dropped away and flattened out into a desert which seemed to have no end. Stubbornly he flew on.

At length Dunyzad said, "I am hungry, Bill."

"Not again!"

"We have been flying for a long time."

He was startled when he saw that the moon was directly overhead. He brought the sled down on a sand dune and they ate the four cantaloupes and drank water from one of the *kullehs*. Beyond them the desert seemed to stretch away forever, and the thought crossed his mind that perhaps the whole planet, with the exception of the valley and the oasis-dotted desert, was dead. He tried to drive it away, but it held its ground, and finally he accepted it as a tentative fact.

He looked at the moon again. It had moved a considerable distance past zenith. There was no longer any reason to prolong the nocturnal journey, and the sooner they went back the way they had come, the better. After they reached the valley he would fly over the mountains and search for the oasis he and Dunyzad had emerged above. It would be easy to find because it was close to the lake. He would then resume his attacks on the Veil. Before he headed for the desert, though, he would stop off at the cave. He doubted if he could bring himself to take any of the treasure, but there was no reason why Dunyzad couldn't help herself.

Lifting the sled, he turned it around and started back. He wasn't altogether certain of the return course, but the control board, which had logged the nighttime trip, was, so he let the automatic pilot take over.

The moon set long before they reached the valley. He put the sled back on manual. The eastern sky grew gray as they flew over the city. Looking down, he saw signs of life at the bottom of the "blue lake." People had come out into the streets and were hurrying toward the square. He saw no sign of the Jinn. Soon someone should turn the blue light off. Unless the Jinn, for mysterious reasons of their own, left it on all the time.

"Look, Bill!" Dunyzad cried. "A rukh!"

It had streaked down from the mountains and was zooming toward them over the valley. He wondered if it was the same one that had seized the sled yesterday. No matter. He hit the emergency time-jump key and bright sunlight exploded around the sled. Dunyzad gasped. The rukh must have returned to its perch, for the sky was empty now.

When he spotted the cave's mouth he headed straight for it. A moment later he wished he hadn't, for he heard the whinny of a horse, but by then it was too late to alter the sled's trajectory or to stop it in time. Obviously the thieves had just arrived, and if he hadn't jumped the sled ahead in time probably he and Dunyzad would have seen them riding up the mountainside. In avoiding Scylla, he had encountered Charybdis.

In his desperate attempt to avoid hitting any of the horses he almost tipped the sled over before he finally found room to land. His finger was on its way to the emergency time-jump key, but it never reached its destination, for two thieves leaped upon him. He clawed in his pocket for his icer, but his seat belt thwarted him. The thieves had alredy seized Dunyzad, and the things she was screaming at them made the things she had screamed at him when he was carrying her across the Sultan's courtyard seem mild by comparison. He made a final frenzied effort to pull his icer from his pocket. He would have succeeded if something hard and heavy hadn't come down on the top of his head and brought his efforts to a sudden end.

IX

'Ali Baba

Billings' head ached, and his eyes, when he first opened them, refused to focus. But he could hear and smell well enough, and the sounds and the smell that reached his ears and nose led him at first to believe he was at a volunteer firemen's convention.

Gradually the double images came together and he was able to distinguish the firemen. All of them wore dirty burnooses with the hoods thrown back, and all of them were drinking out of big earthenware cups which they kept refilling at intervals by dipping them into a big earthenware jar that stood nearby. His nose had already told him that they were drinking beer. They had even created a bar of sorts by aligning the bales of silk and were standing on either side of it.

Billings counted fourteen of them.

One of them was telling a dirty joke. He had a long nose and mean little eyes. When he finished, the others laughed uproariously. "By Allah! you could make a camel laugh, Ibrahim!" one of them exclaimed.

Ibrahim refilled his cup from the jar and started to tell another.

Dunny! Billings thought. Where was Dunny?

He discovered that she was sitting beside him. They were propped against the rear wall of the treasure chamber and their hands were tied behind them and their feet were bound. There was a third party present. He was sitting on the other side of Dunyzad and at first Billings thought he was one of the firemen, because he too wore a burnoose, and then he saw that he was only a boy, not much older than Dunyzad, and that his feet and ankles were also tied.

"Dunny," Billings said, "are you all right?"

He saw that she had been crying. "Oh Bill, I thought you might be dead!"

Her barrette had vanished, and a lock of her black hair had fallen over her forehead. He tried to reach out and brush it back, only to find, of course, that he couldn't free his hand. "There's nothing to cry about, Dunny. I'm fine." He saw that the third prisoner was looking at him. The boy had big and soulful brown eyes, a round face and long and lustrous black hair. "Dunny, who is that?"

"He is 'Ali Baba. He caught them stealing one of his goats and when he tried to stop them they captured him and brought him here. They are going to hold him for ransom because his father is rich."

"If my father does not pay what they want," 'Ali Baba said, "they are going to quarter me."

'Ali Baba, Billings thought. The name was fresh in his mind because he had just dreamed of an 'Ali Baba night before last—the 'Ali Baba of the Shcherazade story of the Forty Thieves: the one who had said the magic words that opened the door of the treasure cave.

Pure coincidence, of course, 'Ali Baba was probably as common a name in ninth-century Arabia as John Smith was in twenty-first-century America.

"I—I am being held for ransom too," Dunyzad said.

"But why, Dunny?—they don't know who you are."

"I—I told them. I—I got mad when they tied me up and I said I was a Vizier's daughter and that my father worked for the Sultan and that the Sultan would chop off their heads when he caught them."

"Oh boy," Billings said.

"My goat was named Bedr-el-Budur," 'Ali Baba said. "I—I was greatly attached to her and she was greatly attached to me. They—they killed and ate her."

"They are fiends!" Dunyzad said. "Just having their heads cut off will be too good for them!"

"In the morning," 'Ali Baba said, "she would come running to me as soon as I stepped out the door, and I would give her a piece of *kunafeh*. Sometimes, if we had had *kataifs* the night before, I would save one for her. She loved *kataifs*, although it is a peculiar food for a goat to eat. But she was an extraordinary goat."

Billings said, "Since the thieves brought you here they must have brought you through the Veil."

"Yes, although I did not know we had gone through it till I heard one of them say we were in the land of the Jinn, because I was blindfolded."

"But didn't any of them mention the Veil?"

"No. But at one time one of them said, 'Open sesame,' and it was shortly afterward that mention was made that we were in the land of the Jinn."

Billings stared into 'Ali Baba's soulful brown eyes. "Open sesame?"

"It sounded like 'Open sesame.' "

"And the Veil opened?"

"Since I was blindfolded, I do not know."

"Sesame is an oil-grain," Dunyzad said. Bill-

ings could see that she was excited. "But maybe
it is a talismanic word too!"

"What were they talking about before that,
'Ali Baba?" Billings asked.

"They were talking about barley beer, and
then they started talking about barley."

"So if they were talking about one kind of
grain they could easily have started talking about
another."

"But why did one of them say 'Open
sesame'?" Dunyzad demanded.

"I don't know," Billings said.

He strongly suspected that 'Ali Baba had sup-
plied the word himself, or had mistaken another word for it. But even if he had heard the
word, the phrase made no sense on a realistic
level. In folklore you could open a cave door
by saying "Open sesame," but in real life the
words would have no effect on a space-time
warp.

At this point one of the thieves, who, cup in
hand, was dancing a fireman's jig, whirled
between a pile of silver ingots and a pile of
gold ones and came to a stop in front of the
three prisoners. His face looked as though a
horse had stepped on it a long time ago. "Lo!"
he cried, looking at Billings. "The dog has
awoke!"

Three of the other thieves joined him. One of
them was the one who had been regaling the
bar with blue jokes and who had been ad-

dressed as Ibrahim, one had only one eye and one had buckteeth the color of turnips. Judging from the laughter that had attended Ibrahim's jokes—it had been sycophantic as well as uproarious—he was the thieves' leader.

He stepped forward and looked down on Billings with his mean little eyes. "Tonight, dog, you will show me how to fly your magic carpet."

Billings had already guessed why they had not dispatched him at once. He made no comment.

"After he shows you, shall we feed him to the rukhs, Ibrahim?" Turnip Teeth asked.

"Perhaps we should quarter him instead," said Horsehoof Face.

"Why not give him to the *ghuls*?" suggested One Eye.

A discussion followed during which Billings' imminent future was mapped out along various routes, each of them sanguinary. Listening to the exchange of inspirational ideas, Billings learned that Turnip Teeth's name was Bedawi, Horsehoof Face's Ja'fir, and One Eye's 'Ajib.

Dunyzad was also listening. At length she leaned forward, and Billings saw that her jaw was thrust forth the way it had been when she wanted to take on the Jinn. "If you so much as touch him," she said, "I will tell the Sultan to hang each of you up by your thumbs till you are in such excessive torture you will pray to Allah for the Sultan to behead you! You evil-

smelling Bedouins! You sons of she-dogs! You
eaters of offal! You worthless scoundrels! You
heaps of dromedary dung!''

She went on and on and on. Billings was
appalled by some of the things she said. As for
the thieves, they just stood there with their
mouths open. Ibrahim was the first to get back
his voice. "Ja'fir!'' he shouted in a desperate
attempt to regain his aplomb, "go get another
jar of buzah! The one we have been imbibing
from is almost empty!''

Ja'fir hotfooted it across the chamber to the
tunnel and Ibrahim, Bedawi and 'Ajib returned
to the bar.

They weren't quite drunk enough yet to cope
with Dunyzad.

Soon they would be.

Although no one asked him to, 'Ali Baba gave a
brief rundown of the thieves' life-style, as he
had gleaned it from their conversations and
from his observations before they had blindfolded him. "They do not steal from the poor,''
he said, "and this is understandable because
what would there be to steal? But they call
themselves the Saviors of the Poor, and the
poor people love them and give them their
choice of their most beautiful daughters. When
they are not stealing they mask themselves as
merchants and craftsmen. Ibrahim has a bazaar
in Baghdad and Ja'fir is a successful tailor. He

sells female slaves on the side. They hide what they steal until there is enough of it to bring to the cave. When they make the journey they travel by night and sleep in tents by day. They have eight extra horses. Six of them are for carrying what they have stolen and the two others are for carrying jars of *buzah*. You can see from all the riches surrounding us," 'Ali Baba concluded, "how much they are benefiting the poor."

"The foul, filthy dogs!" Dunyzad said.

Billings, whose headache had gotten no better, said nothing.

'Ali Baba got back to the subject of his goat, and he told how he had raised her from a kid and how, sometimes, he used to take her with him when he went to the village to buy food. People thought he was crazy, he said, but he hadn't cared. Bedr-el-Budur had been the most beautiful goat in all the land, and there would never be another one like her.

When he got through talking Dunyzad told him all about her and Billings, about how Billings had stolen her from the Sultan's palace and how they had set forth on his magic carpet for his own palace and how they had inadvertently passed through the Veil; about the Jinn and about how the rukh had thought they were going to damage its egg and had borne them off to the mountains and how they had escaped from it and found the cave, and about the val-

ley and the City of Brass. She then proceeded
to tell 'Ali Baba the same story about the Veil
she had told Billings, after which she launched
into a detailed description of her ring, which,
fortunately, the thieves had been unable to pull
from her finger. Afterwards she told him about
the Great Battle which Suleyman had waged
against the Jinn, and of which 'Ali Baba presumably had never heard; how Suleyman had
imprisoned all of the Jinn who wouldn't embrace the faith in brass bottles and had thrown
the bottles into the Sea of El-Karkar, and had
let the ones who embraced the faith go back to
the land of the Jinn. And 'Ali Baba sat there
eating up every word, looking at her the same
way, Billings suspected, he had once looked at
Bedr-el-Budur, his goat, with adoration written
all over his face and shining in his eyes.

Meanwhile the thieves got drunker and
drunker, and the sunlight, which had been shining vertically through the fissure in the cave's
ceiling, took on greater and greater inclination
as the afternoon progressed.

Dunyzad continued to talk and 'Ali Baba continued to listen. She was now telling him one
of her sister's tales. "The Story of the Fisherman."
As was to be expected, it had a Jinni in it.
Billings became disgusted. Didn't either she or
'Ali Baba realize the extent of the fix the three
of them were in? And how could she keep on
talking ad infinitum when she hadn't had a

drop of water to drink all day? He knew that
she was telling the story to entertain him as
well as 'Ali Baba, for she kept glancing his
way, but it seemed to him she ought to know
enough to draw the line somewhere.

When night at last fell, one of the thieves
lighted the lamps in the wall niches and the
beer blast went on unabated. Not long afterward Ibrahim and Ja'fir staggered to the rear of
the cave. Ja'fir had a long-bladed knife in his
hand and Billings thought for a moment that
they were going to release him so he could give
Ibrahim a magic-carpet flying lesson. He hoped
his right hand would not be too numb to handle his icer. He knew it was still in his trousers
pocket because he could feel it against his leg.
Either the thieves had not noticed it, or, if they
had, had written it off as a cheap piece of
nondescript jewelry. But it was not the magic
carpet that was on Ibrahim's mind, it was
Dunyzad, for by this time he had drunk enough
to cope with her. Or so he thought. He pointed
to her and told Ja'fir to cut her bonds.

Drooling, Ja'fir did so. Ibrahim leaned over
her. "On your feet, daughter of a dog! The
Saviors of the Poor need a dancing girl!"

Dunyzad looked up at him as though she
were gazing into a pit. "You wish me to *dance*?"

"With your belly," Ja'fir drooled.

She rubbed her wrists and then her ankles
till the circulation came back, then she stood

up and pushed Ja'fir and Ibrahim away. "Very well then, I will dance," she said, and to Billings' dismay, and to 'Ali Baba's too, judging from the sick look on his face, she whirled off toward the bar.

X

The Superjinni

The chamber, if you discounted the treasure, now had the aspect of a twenty-first-century Go Go Girl bar after a firemen's parade. All of the firemen had moved to one side of the bar so they could see the Go Go Girl better, and in between chug-a-lugs were whistling and shouting their brains out.

Billings' and 'Ali Baba's view of the proceedings was only partly cut off by two piles of ingots, and Billings was shocked when he saw Dunyzad begin to wriggle her belly like a professional belly dancer as she moved about the floor. Then, to his horror and to the accompaniment of shouts of encouragement from the thieves, she kicked off her slippers and began to take her bloomers off. His horror abated somewhat when he saw that she had a pink pair on underneath. But suppose she took those off too?

Passing one of the piles of household items, she picked up the elongated lamp she had called Billings' attention to yesterday and began to use it as a cymbal. Then he saw that instead of striking it she was rubbing it.

One of the thieves ran out from the bar and tried to grab her. She hit him over the head with the lamp so hard that he dropped to his knees. The rest of the thieves guffawed as he crawled back to the bar.

She resumed rubbing the lamp.

Surely she can't be so naïve as to believe a good Jinni will pop out of nowhere and save the day! Billings thought. All that nonsense about her ring was bad enough without this!

Then he saw that there was another fireman standing at the bar. A great big linebacker of a fireman at least ten feet tall, with broad shoulders and a big square face and a jaw that looked as though it had been sculpted out of concrete and a pair of gray eyes that had mini-tornadoes whirling in their depths. He was wearing a crimson silk vest that left his huge chest bare, a pair of sky-blue silk bloomers and yard-long Persian slippers with high heels. With each breath he expelled, smoke shot forth from his nostrils.

The consternation that had come into the thieves' eyes outmatched that which had come into Billings', and it was tinged with awe. Dunyzad had stopped rubbing the lamp and was staring at the big linebacker too, and it was clear that she didn't believe her eyes any more than Billings believed his. He had been right: she had not really believed a Jinni would appear. She had only hoped one would.

"Thou—thou must be the Slave of the Lamp," she said in a weak voice.

The big linebacker walked toward her across the room. It only took him two and a half steps to reach her, and he stood over her like a tall tree. His nostrils were quivering and the mini-tornadoes in his eyes had multiplied and he was almost shaking with rage, "Let it be known at once, damsel," he said in a tremendous voice, "that contrary to that which your wretched folklore says of me, I am not a slave. I am one of the Transcendent Jinn, and my name is Dahish. Out of the kindness of my heart I have assigned myself the task of assisting mortals such as yourself who have come into possession of the Lamp of the Aesthetic and who, finding themselves in dire difficulty, have transmitted a distress signal by rubbing it. I am, in simple language, a Superjinni who can move Heaven and Earth by the mere command of his voice."

Dunyzad's face had turned pale, but she didn't retreat a single inch. "You may be able to move Heaven and Earth at the mere command of your voice," she said, "but as the holder of the Lamp I can command you."

The big Jinni ground his teeth, but no sparks shot forth. Then he sighed. "It was all my own doing, I suppose. What is it that you wish?"

She pointed to the fourteen thieves. "Those foul-smelling Bedouins are holding 'Ali Baba and me for ransom, and it is their evil intention to do something horrible to Bill after he shows them how to fly his magic carpet. I wish you to drive them away."

The Superjinni faced the thieves. All of them had fallen to their knees. "She lies!" Ibrahim cried from his. "We took her and her companions captive so they would not steal the riches for which we have slaved all our miserable lives! It was our intention to free them before we returned to our own land. We are honorable men with wives and children. It is she and her companions who should be driven away!"

Dahish shrugged. "It is she," he pointed out, "who has the Lamp."

"But it is ours!" Ibrahim screamed. "We sto—we bought it in Baghdad and brought it here! It is ours, ours, ours!"

"They are thieves!" Dunyzad spat. "They stole everything in this room!"

Dahish shrugged again. "I do not care what they are. You have commanded me to drive them away. Therefore—"

"Wait," Dunyzad said, and ran over to Ja'fir,

seized his long bladed knife and went over to Billings and 'Ali Baba and cut their bonds. She stuck Ja'fir's knife back in his belt and rejoined the Superjinni. "Very well, Dahish," she said. "Now you can proceed."

Dahish raised his arm and the fourteen thieves vanished.

Dunyzad stared at where they had been. Billings and 'Ali Baba, who had gotten to their feet, stared too. "Where—where did you drive them?" Dunyzad asked.

"I transferred them and their horses to one of the rukhs' nests."

Aghast, she cried, "But I did not tell you to drive their horses away too!"

"They were only cluttering up the cave."

"I did not *want* you to drive them away! And when I commanded you to drive the thieves away I did not mean for you to transfer them to a rukh's nest!"

"Damsel, you should be more specific when you issue a command."

"Well get them and their horses out of the nest at once!"

Dahish sighed. "Very well. It is done."

"Where are they now?"

"They are on a desert thousands of miles away."

"But they'll die there!"

"I thought you wanted them to die."

"I did not want their horses to die!"

"Both they and their horses can find food enough to live on and water to drink."

Billings, who did not in the least believe any of the things that were going on, nevertheless walked over to Dunyzad's side, looked up into Dahish's lofty face and said, "Tell us how we can get back through the Veil."

If Dahish was aware of Billings' presence or had heard what he said, he gave no sign. He stood there like a huge chunk of granite which some crazy sculptor had carved into a statue.

"Dunny," Billings said, "ask him how we can get back through the Veil."

Dunyzad said, "Tell us, Dahish."

"Tell you what?"

"How we can get back through the Veil!"

"I cannot tell you."

"You do not know?"

Dashish ground his teeth. "Of course I know!"

"Then tell us."

"Transcendent Jinn are forbidden to discuss the Veil. Moreover, no one is capable of passing through it except us."

"But we passed through it! The thieves have passed through it time and time again! And even ordinary Jinn can pass through it!"

"No one is supposed to know how but us!"

"I order you to tell me!"

"I refuse. If you believe that ordinary Jinn know how, go to the City of Brass and ask Ed-Dimiryat."

"Who is Ed-Dimiryat?"

"He is the leader of the terrestrial Jinn. May I depart now, damsel?"

"Assuming Ed-Dimiryat knows, suppose he refuses to tell me?"

Dahish threw up his hands. "Damsel, you will have to talk him into it. May I depart?"

Dunyzad sighed. "Very well. But I may need you again."

The Superjinni vanished.

"Oh boy," Billings said, and sat down on the floor.

Dunyzad laid down the lamp and began looking at some of the new articles of loot which the thieves had brought. 'Ali Baba joined her. More gold, more silver, more jewelry, more silk. "Dunyzad," 'Ali Baba said, "if we could transport all of these wondrous items to Baghdad, think of the tremendous bazaar we could open!"

"But why would we need to open a bazaar, 'Ali? We would merely be using riches to get riches when already we would have all the riches we would ever need."

"That is true," 'Ali Baba said.

Dunyzad came over to where Billings was sitting, 'Ali Baba at her heels. "Does your head hurt, Bill?"

"Only a little." Having at last gotten reality back into focus, he arose to his feet. "Dunny, put your bloomers back on!"

She picked them up and began slipping into them. "I forgot all about them."

"I don't see why you had to take them off in the first place!"

She finished slipping them back on. "It was so the thieves would be paying so much attention to my legs they would not notice me rubbing the lamp. Besides, I had another pair on."

"Those pink ones are part of your underwear!"

"But the thieves did not know that, Bill."

"The pink ones became you exceedingly," 'Ali Baba said.

Billings glared at him. "Never mind whether they became her or not! Did the thieves bring any water with them?"

"I believe they brought just *buzah*."

"We could drink some of that, Bill," Dunyzad said. "It will be better than nothing. I am so thirsty I can hardly talk."

Billings found this hard to believe.

"Not only would it quench our thirst," 'Ali Baba said, "but it would relax us too."

Billings put his foot down. "No." Just from the smell of the barley beer (which permeated every cubic inch of the treasure chamber) he knew it would make him sick, and he was certain it would make Dunyzad and 'Ali Baba sick too. "What we'll do instead is fly down into the valley and drink some water out of the stream. But first we'll have something to eat if the thieves didn't steal the rations. And maybe, just maybe, those *kullehs* I filled from the stream didn't tip over, in which case we can quench our thirst right away."

He found his flashlight, which the thieves had overlooked, and 'Ali Baba took one of the lamps out of one of the wall niches. Then they made their way through the tunnel to the outer chamber. Dahish had not lied about transferring the horses, and except for the sled the chamber was empty.

The first thing Billings did was check the sled. Since Ibrahim had planned on taking flying lessons he didn't think the thieves would have damaged it and he found they had not. Nor were the batteries drained, for the auto-control switch had shut the intra-era inertia regulator off fifteen minutes after he brought the sled down. All of the *kullehs*, however, had tipped over and not a drop of water remained in any of them. He checked the contents of the tool-box and the equipment and ration box. Insofar as he could tell, nothing had been taken. Maybe the thieves hadn't been able to work the catches on the lids.

There were three mouths to feed now. He took out a corned-beef-and-cheese for Dunyzad and two wieners-and-beans for himself and 'Ali Baba. They ate by lamplight just within the mouth of the cave, the light of the moon lapping at their feet.

"When are we going to pay Ed-Dimiryat a visit, Bill?" Dunyzad asked.

"Tonight."

"He will tell us how to get back through the Veil. I will force him to."

"With your ring?" 'Ali Baba asked.

"Yes. With my ring."

Her and that darn ring! Billings thought. But he hid his irritation and concentrated on what he was going to do. Although he had his doubts about Ed-Dimiryat, there was a chance that the Jinni, if it existed and if he could find it and if he could communicate with it, would tell him how to get back through the Veil. The chance, at least, was worth taking, even though it necessitated his having to enter the tower. But he didn't tell Dunyzad he wasn't going to take her and 'Ali Baba into the tower with him. He would wait and tell her when they reached the city.

He wished he could leave both of them in the cave, but he didn't dare. It was true that Dahish had made the thieves vanish, but this was no guarantee that they wouldn't reappear. He simply couldn't risk letting the two teenagers fall back into their hands.

He had finished eating and so had they. He stood up. "We might as well get started."

"But we have not loaded the treasure on yet, Bill," Dunyzad said.

"We'll come back for it."

"And the magic lamp. I wish to take that too."

"You can get it when we come back."

She seated herself on the sled. " 'Ali, you'll have to sit on that box behind her. Hang on tight to the back of her seat."

'Ali's face was pale in the lamplight as he stepped up on the sled. "There is nothing to be afraid of, 'Ali," Dunyzad reassured him. "Magic carpets are fun."

"I am not in the least afraid," 'Ali Baba said, sitting down behind her and gripping the back of her seat so hard that his knuckles almost jumped out of his flesh.

Billings left the lamp on and stepped up and seated himself beside Dunyzad. He fastened his safety belt and checked to see whether she had fastened hers. Satisfied, he pressed the hover button and activated the intra-era inertia regulator. "Here we go," he said, and turned the sled around and guided it out into the moonlight.

XI
The Rotunda

He brought the sled down near the bank of the stream almost in the same spot where he had landed it last night. "Watch out for ghuls, 'Ali," Dunyzad said as she stepped down to the ground. "Especially ghulehs."

"*Ghuls?* Oh, I am not afraid of them."

"Watch out for them anyway," Billings said.

After they had drunk from the stream he filled the *kullehs*. This time, he filled all six. "Should we take another bath, Bill?" Dunyzad asked as he was placing them on the sled.

"Not tonight."

"Let me borrow your comb then so I can comb my hair."

While she was combing it on the bank of the stream 'Ali Baba moved close to Billings and said, "The locks of her brow are as dark as night, while her forehead shines like the gleam of the moon."

"You mean Dunny?"

"Never before has it been my good fortune to behold a damsel as marvelous as she."

Billings just looked at him.

"Shall we pick some fruit, Bill?" Dunyzad asked, returning to his side and handing him back his comb.

"All right."

After they entered the orchard she climbed up on Billings' shoulders beneath a cantaloupe-laden limb. He could see that 'Ali Baba desperately wanted her to climb up on his. Just what I needed to make my day complete, Billings thought. A lovesick schoolboy!

"Catch, 'Ali," Dunyzad cried, tossing down a cantaloupe. It slipped through 'Ali Baba's hands. She tossed down several more, all of which he managed to grab before they hit the ground. "Is that enough, Bill?"

Billings was staring up into the branches above her head. "Dunny, is that the same owl we saw last night?"

It sat among the leaves, gazing down at them with round, lens-like eyes. "It looks like the same one."

"Can you reach it?"

"But it will bite me, Bill!"

"I don't think so." He hunched up his shoulders to give her more height. "See if you can grab it."

Her extended fingers touched the owl's feet. Promptly it winged up among the branches and disappeared. Dunyzad jumped down to the ground. "Why did you want me to grab it?"

"I don't think it's a real owl."

"But it *looked* like a real owl."

"I think it's a mechanical one and that the Jinn were watching us through its eyes and listening to us with its ears."

Both Dunyzad and 'Ali Baba were staring at him. "The Jinn probably use it to spy on the people who work in the orchard, and maybe the people think it's a real owl. But it's not. It's a remote-controlled mechanical device with lenses for eyes, transmitters for ears, and a brain consisting of tiny tubes and wires."

"That is impossible," Dunyzad said.

"Completely impossible," said 'Ali Baba.

Billings was exasperated. "Why is it the two of you can take the Jinn in your stride, and the *ghuls* too, and still can't accept a simple device such as a mechanical owl? Come on, let's get out of the orchard. There are probably more of them in the trees."

They carried the cantaloupes back to the sled and Billings, whose pocketknife the thieves had not deemed worth stealing, cut three of them into quarters. They ate sitting on the bank of the stream. Billings kept glancing at the opposite bank, but the ghuleh who had conned him last night did not reappear.

Were the damn things vampires? he wondered.

They very well might be. It was silly to say that there were no such things when you were in a milieu that sported ordinary Jinn, Transcendent Jinn, and birds as big as superjets.

After he and Dunyzad and 'Ali Baba finished their cantaloupes he put the rest of the fruit into the equipment and ration box. Dunyzad was already at his side. "Are we going to the city now, Bill?"

"As soon as you and 'Ali Baba climb on board."

"Do you think the Jinn found out from the owl that we are coming?"

"I thought you didn't believe what I said about the owl."

"It is hard for me to believe. But I know that what you said must be true, even though I cannot understand how it can be."

"All they found out through the owl," Billings said, "was where we are, and since none of us said anything about the city, they can't very well know we're going there. But that doesn't mean they won't be on the watch for us. Come on, 'Ali—climb on board."

*   *   *

He lifted the sled straight up. The blue glow of the City of Brass vied in the distance with the argent light of the moon. He pointed the prow toward the glow and put the intra-era inertia regulator on full speed. He hoped Ed-Dimiryat would prove to be a jovial Jinni and would not turn out to be an 'Efrit.

By this time 'Ali Baba had gotten over his fear of flying, and he and Dunyzad began conversing as the sled sailed over the argent fields and orchards and the winding tinsel of the stream. Before long he got back to the subject of his goat, and Dunyzad made sympathetic noises as he again recounted how he had brought the animal up from a kid. Then he began talking about his father's farm, and said he hoped that after they got back through the Veil Dunyzad would come for a visit some day. He was aware, he went on, that she belonged to the Emir Bill, and that were love to mature between them, she would become his bride, but love, he said, was not a quality one could put one's finger upon, and oftentimes it deftly eluded its pursuers and hid in the brambles alongside the road of life. Were this to occur in the present instance, it was to be hoped that Dunyzad would cast her beautiful eyes in his direction.

Billings glanced at him sideways but said nothing.

As they neared the city he slowed the sled. The moon seemed to have paused in its nocturnal voyage directly above the apex of the tower, and its light, not quite outdone by the blue radiance bathing the buildings of the city proper, turned the tower itself into a cold metal flame. As had been the case last night, there was no sign of life, and the only light to be seen, other than the blue radiance, was the same dim light he had noticed last night in the tower's only window.

He slowed the sled to a crawl and edged it over to the window, then locked it on hover. The window was a vertical slot in the thick wall. He tried to see what lay beyond it, but the dim light told him nothing. Unfastening his safety belt, he turned toward Dunyzad. "Dunny, I'm going inside, but before I go I want to show you how to fly the magic carpet in case something goes wrong."

Her eyes had gone wide with disbelief. "*You are going inside without me?*"

"Dunny, I can't risk taking you with me. I'm sure nothing'll go wrong, but—"

"But Bill, I have the ring!"

He patted his trousers pocket. "I have a talisman here of my own and—"

"Without the seal of Suleyman you will be helpless against the Jinn!"

"No I won't be." He pointed to the control board. "Do you see that little green button? When you want to go ahead you push it down. Those two little buttons just below it are for

left and right changes of direction. If you want
to go to the left you press the left-hand one
down, just a little if you want to veer only a
little and harder if you want to make a sharper
turn. You do the same thing with the right-
hand one when you want to change your direction to the right. The little red button below
them is for bringing the sled to a halt. That
lever to the right of the buttons regulates
velocity. When you push it forward you go
faster and when you pull it backward you go
slower." He paused. She had folded her arms
across her chest and was staring straight ahead.
"Dunny, pay attention!"

"I do not wish to know how to fly your
wretched carpet and if you do not take me into
the tower with you I shall never speak to you
again!"

"I can't take you with me!"

"You can too!"

Desperately he turned toward 'Ali Baba. "Do
you think you can fly it?"

"Of course," 'Ali Baba said.

Grimly Billings went through the instructions
again and told 'Ali all else he would need to
know in order to manipulate the inertia regulator and the anti-grav. When he finished he asked
'Ali if he understood, wondering how he possibly could have when so many of the words he
had used were English. But 'Ali merely nodded
his head and said, "Yes, I can fly it now."

"All right. I want you and Dunny to wait here till I get back, but if I'm not back by the time the moon sets, or if the Jinn attack you, I want you to leave at once."

"Where—where shall we go, Emir Bill?"

"Back to the cave. But you won't need to leave, because I'll be back in no time at all and if any of the Jinn attack you I'll turn them into icicles." He looked at Dunyzad. She still sat there staring straight ahead with her arms folded across her chest. Well let her be mad at him! he didn't care. He drew his icer out of his pocket, stepped from the sled to the ledge of the aperture and entered the tower.

He knew he was taking a crazy chance, that at least a dozen Jinn might be waiting for him in the dimness—far more than he could quick-freeze in time to do himself any good. But the big room in which he found himself proved to be deserted. It was also devoid of objects of any kind, except for a big brass bottle suspended from the ceiling on a trio of brass chains and hanging about seven feet above the floor. The ceiling was so high that the room had more of the aspect of a closet than a room. It and the walls and the floor were brass too, or, if not brass, an alloy that looked exactly like it.

Opposite the window was a door which had been left ajar. Approaching it, he saw that it was a good fifteen feet in height but only about

three wide. It, too, was brass, and judging from
its thickness it must have weighed at least half
a ton. But it swung inward easily enough when
he pulled it open the rest of the way, and did
not emit so much as a single squeak.

Stepping through the doorway he found himself on a landing which, a short distance to his
left, slanted downward and became a ramp.
Opposite him a buffed brass wall, broken by
another enormous door, bisected the entire top
section of the tower. To his right, another buffed
brass wall marked the interior of the outside
wall.

Like the room, the landing was deserted.

He became aware of a pungent smell. It had
been present also in the room he had just left,
but he hadn't taken conscious note of it. In a
way it reminded him of the acrid smell electric
wires give off when they are shorted.

B.O.?

He now took conscious note of something
else: the dim light which had bathed the room
and which bathed the landing and the ramp
had no apparent source. But this was no big
deal. Photon dispersal was a common form of
illumination way back before the twenty-first
century.

But if it was available, why didn't the Jinn
use it to illuminate the city? Why, instead, did
they bathe the buildings and the streets with a

light so deeply blue it concealed more than it revealed?

The source of that light, he was sure, lay beyond the wall across the landing. He went over and tried the enormous door. It would not budge.

Were there Jinn behind it? he wondered.

He decided to gamble that there were not, and keeping his right forearm at right angles to his side so that his icer would be in position in case he needed to use it in a hurry, he started down the ramp. Almost at once it cut sharply to the left and then descended in a gently inclined spiral through a wide well in the tower's center. On his left, a high brass wall prevented him from looking down to the bottom of the well; on his right, the inside wall of the tower matched the curvature of the ramp.

Presently he came to another huge door. He pushed on it and it swung inward as easily as though it weighed half a pound instead of half a ton. He peered into the room it gave access to. Except for the absence of a window it was exactly like the one he had just quitted, and hanging from its lofty ceiling on a trio of brass chains was a big brass bottle exactly like the one he had just seen.

He was tempted to take the bottle down and look inside, but it was too high above his head for him to handle.

The door was the first of many, and appar-

ently none were locked (there was no visible
mechanism by which they could have been),
but after pushing open three more and finding
three more identical chambers and three more
identical brass bottles hanging from the ceil-
ings he concluded that he was wasting his time
and tried no more.

At length the long series of evenly spaced
doors gave way to a smooth, uninterrupted surface and not long afterward the ramp leveled
out into a straight corridor. He knew then that
he had reached the ground floor, and slowed
his pace. Since he had not yet encountered a
Jinni, they must all be in bed, and the corridor
might very well lead to their bedrooms.

Presently he came to its end, and found himself confronted by a door so big it made the
others seem small. But it was no less cooper-
ative, and shoving it open, he stepped cau-
tiously into a huge chamber.

No, not huge—vast. The highest point of the
domed ceiling was at least fifty feet above the
floor, and suspended from the ceiling's center
on three heavy brass chains was a brass bottle
twice as large as the ones he had seen in the
rooms.

He knew he was no longer inside the tower,
that he had entered an adjoining dome which
the blue light must have obscured when he
looked down at the city from the time sled.

The air was exceedingly warm and dry. It

was as though a hot desert wind had blown
into the rotunda and had been unable to escape.
The acrid smell he had noticed in the tower
and which, he remembered, he had also noticed when the Jinn had paraded around the
oasis, seemed to have intensified.

Like the rooms, the rotunda was devoid of
furniture. But not of equipment. What appeared
to be a huge console stood against the opposite
wall, and above it was a big display board
consisting of tier after tier of postage-stamp-
sized screens arranged in the form of a square.
The console gave forth a brasslike sheen, and
the rotunda, discounting the flatness of the floor,
resembled the interior of a huge brass bubble.

The integrated light was brighter here. Billings walked through it to the middle of the
room so he could see the screens better. He had
thought he saw people depicted in them, but
he still wasn't close enough to tell. He walked
the rest of the way across the rotunda to the
console, only to have its upper edge cut off his
view.

The console's face was blank and provided
no hand or footholds. Favoring his ankle, he
jumped up and gripped the edge and pulled
himself up on top. There was a small screen
and a solitary keyboard on the upper surface
and he knew that he had found the console's
control board. His new eminence allowed him
to see several of the vertical screens clearly.

Concentrating on one of them, he saw a tiny room which had two doors and which contained a tiny bed, a tiny couch, a tiny table and a tiny chair. Seated on the tiny chair, his elbows resting on the tiny table, was a tiny man with a bald, domelike head. He was unquestionably alive, unquestionably deep in thought and unquestionably a mere fraction of his actual size. From the ceiling a wire ran down to an electrode which was attached to the top of his head. His clothing consisted of a tunic of coarse cloth.

Billings looked at two of the other screens. Both depicted identical rooms furnished with identical furniture, but only one of them was inhabited. This time the inhabitant was a woman. Her head was also bald and domelike and she wore a tunic similar to the man's. She was lying on the couch with her eyes closed, and a wire ran down from the ceiling to an electrode on her head.

The rooms looked like cells, and indeed, since the city was a prison what else could they be? But Billings knew that only a very small percentage of the prisoners were confined in them, and that those that were must be unique in some way.

He lowered himself back down to the floor and moved a short distance away from the console and turned and looked up at the screens.

He had never before seen a human computer, but he was certain he was looking at one now.

Was it growing warmer in the room, or was his imagination playing tricks on him? And what was that odd humming noise behind him?

Turning around, he saw the Jinni.

XII

Ed-Dimiryat

The creature standing before him was at least thirty feet tall. Its legs looked like a pair of brass pillars, its feet resembled the cornerstones of a large building, its arms brought to mind a pair of giant piston rods and its hands were as big as unabridged dictionaries. These were its most redeeming physical characteristics. On a more personal and less redeeming note, its head looked like a brass dome, its eyes glowed like gasoline lanterns, its nose was shaped like a French horn, its ears stuck out like TV antennae and its mouth made Billings think of a rock-crusher.

How in the world had it ever crept up behind him without making a sound?

But it *had* made a sound. It had hummed.

A few moments ago it had been a pillar of

smoke, or dust, or whatever Jinn in their untransformed state were comprised of. But it had not entered the rotunda. It had already been in the rotunda.

The truth stretched his imagination, but he confronted it. The Jinni had come out of the brass bottle.

That being so, each of the brass bottles in the tower might have a Jinni in it.

Did they sleep in the damn things?

"Allow me to introduce myself," the one standing before him said. It spoke in twenty-first-century English, and although the words were clear they sounded as though they had been shoveled out of a gravel pit. "I'm Ed-Dimiryat. We were keeping an eye on you and your female companion after you came through the Veil, and then, unaccountably, you disappeared. But I was certain that sooner or later you'd pay us a visit. We've already learned from our owls that your name is Bill. Your alacrity in perceiving their true nature took me somewhat by surprise."

By this time Billings had regained his aplomb. He hadn't altogether lost it, since the Jinni was within icer range and could easily be put out of action. "It was pretty obvious," he said in a voice loud enough to reach Ed-Dimiryat's "ears."

"I'm what the female who came with you through the Veil would call a Marid," Ed-Dimiryat went on, "but let me assure you that the evil ascribed to Jinn of such denomination is purely a product of folklore. You've no doubt noted that I'm addressing you in your own language, but this is true only in the sense that the words I'm speaking are filtered through an oral translation field before they leave my mouth. My ears are similarly equipped, and I can understand whatever you may say regardless of whichever of the ancient terrestrial languages you speak it in. . . . Do you have to keep staring at me as though I were some kind of monster? We Jinn try to make ourselves as human-looking as we can, but it's an extremely difficult task."

"Can't you make yourself any smaller?" Billings shouted.

"I can condense my present shape a little more—yes." The Marid lost about ten feet in height; now it was only about twenty feet tall. "There, that should be more in keeping with your parameters."

"How come the Transcendent Jinn can make themselves look exactly like humans and you can't?"

"You saw one of the Transcendent Jinn?"

"Yes. His name was Dahish. He—"

"Why do you say 'he'? Jinn are sexless."

"Because he looked like a big linebacker. We asked him how we could get back through the Veil, but he said that Transcendent Jinn were forbidden to discuss the Veil and that we should ask you."

" 'Transcendent,' " Ed-Dimiryat said disdainfully, "is an adjective which they apply to themselves. They think that because they can appear and disappear that they're superior to the rest of us. They won't have anything to do with us ordinary Jinn, and recently some of them have dropped out of Jinn life. Dahish is one of the worst. To show its contempt for us ordinary Jinn it's actually gone so far as to reduce itself to the status of slave by putting itself on call to any human being who happens to come into possession of the 'Lamp of the Aesthetic,' its name for a camouflaged signaling device which it left in the land of Men and which one of you creatures must have got hold of. That female companion of yours, I'll bet!"

"Dahish made it very clear," Billings said, "that he is not a slave."

"Naturally it wouldn't admit the fact to mere mortals. But I venture to say it did exactly what was asked of it."

"Up to when we asked him how to get back through the Veil. He then told us to go to the City of Brass and ask you."

"I find it odd," Ed-Dimiryat said, nicely skirting the subject of the Veil, "that you haven't as yet expressed any curiosity as to the provenance of beings such as myself and Dahish."

"It's been obvious to me for some time that you come from another planet."

"It's the sixteenth world of a star to which your astronomers have given the name of 'Alioth.' The Jinn have been on Earth for hundreds and hundreds of years and have rehabilitated most of the terrestrials and transferred them to younger worlds. This particular Rehabilitation Center is the last of its kind and all the other Jinn except those of us here in the Center and a few 'transcendent' ones like Dahish, who have wandered off somewhere, have gone home. Once the terrestrials in the Center have been rehabilitated they too will be transferred to one of the younger worlds and our task on Earth will be done."

"This is a *Rehabilitation* Center?"

"I can't think of a better name for it."

Billings could, and already had, but he saw no point in provoking an argument. "Just why did you take it into your heads to 'rehabilitate' the peoples of Earth?"

"In their former state they were a menace to our civilization, and not only that, their planet was dying. You can see for yourself that it's almost dead now. The area we occupy is one of the last of the inhabitable ones. The closest Rehabilitation Center to this one is hundreds of miles away, but naturally it's deserted now."

"You brought the rukhs with you?"

"They are our pets."

"But you had to establish a whole ecosystem for them!"

"It posed no problem, for we had plenty of human labor."

"The ghuls—did you bring them too?"

"The ghuls," Ed-Dimiryat said, "are unhappy products of human immortality experiments conducted long before our arrival. Not only did we not bring them, we've been unable to do anything about them."

"Where are your spaceships?"

The Marid's laughter reverberated throughout the rotunda, and for a moment Billings thought he was in a cement factory. "The Jinn graduated from spaceships millennia ago!"

"Then how did you get here?"

"We bent space—and time too, since you can't bend one without bending the other—and passed through the warp."

Billings was awed. "The warp—is it still in existence?"

"Of course. We won't eliminate it till we leave."

Billings had thought he was pretty smart. He was part of a race of people who had conquered time—not that the conquest had done anyone except the historical researchers and the owners of history-related companies like Animanikins, Inc. much good. But here before him stood a being whose race had conquered space and time, and had bent them as though they were a pin!

He changed the subject to give his mind a chance to clear. "Those people in those cells," he said, pointing toward the screens. "Are they part of your 'rehabilitation program'?"

"They're geniuses whom we've culled from among the terrestrials. We use them primarily for computation purposes, but we also use them to solve the ordinary problems which occasionally arise in our on-going program for the betterment of them and their less intelligent brethren."

"They're geniuses and you keep them locked up in cells?"

"Those aren't cells! They're thinking chambers. And the people in them have all the comforts of home. All their meals are served to them and at regular intervals they're allowed to fraternize. Not only that, they have days off during which we let them go for walks in the valley."

"They look like they're locked in."

"Well it may look that way," Ed-Dimiryat said with a trace of irritation in its voice, "but I assure you they are not, although I'll admit they're confined to their quarters. But aside from the fact that the other terrestrials are allowed to go out into the streets during the day they're not one whit worse off than they are. Post-hypnotic suggestion has rendered all our charges submissive to the incarcerative rays of the blue light that bathes the entire compound. There's a valid rason for such restriction," Ed-Dimiryat went on, "for even the inhabitants of a Rehabilitation Center aren't above trying to escape, and escape in the present instance would be self-negating, since the escapees would fall victim either to the rukhs, which, although they're not normally carnivorous, aren't above dining on flesh if it's readily available, or the *ghuls.* The guards which are posted in the valley, in fact, are there as much to protect the terrestrials as to keep them from escaping. But with respect to the cerebralities—the thinkers—there's an even more valid reason for keeping them in tow. Their superior intelligence has brought them to the plateau of humanistic maturity, but unfortunately it has also accentuated an atavistic element common in the human psyche. To put it simply, they're geniuses one moment and aggressive and vindictive and irresponsible children the next, and if we were to allow them to run loose, our entire program would be turned into a shambles."

"Is that why you televise them?—so you can keep an eye on them?"

"No. So long as the blue light is on, they remain docile. The screens merely enable us to tell whether they're concentrating or just pretending to."

"I can hardly see them from this far away."

"That's because you're not a Jinni. And now,"

Ed-Dimiryat said, "I'd like to ask a question. It's evident from the nature of your vehicle that you're from a terrestrial time period far in advance of the one you departed from when you came through the . . . ah . . . Veil. Just how far in advance is it?"

"Twelve centuries. I came back in time to abduct Dunyzad. We have a deal going on where we make animated copies of Very Important Past Persons. The copies are put on exhibit and people pay lots of money to come and see them and hear them talk."

"May I ask why you abducted her?"

"I—I abducted her by mistake. I was supposed to abduct her sister."

"What makes her sister so important?"

"She tells stories to the Sultan that people in my century like to listen to. The stories will be on tape, of course, but it'll seem as though her facsimile is actually relating them, and the facsimile will be so lifelike it'll be indistinguishable from the real thing."

"And you want to get this . . ah . . . Dunyzad back through the Veil so you can make the exchange and take her sister to the future?"

"Well no, not exactly. I want to take her to the future first so a facsimile can be made of her."

"Why in the world would anyone want to make a facsimile of someone like her?"

The Marid, for some reason, had it in for

Dunyzad, and it was with difficulty that Billings held on to his temper. "Because she's important too!" he said. "But the main thing is to get her back through the Veil to her own day and age. I've tried to get us back through the same way we came through in the first place, but so far I've had no luck. That's why I've come here to ask your help."

Ed-Dimiryat gazed down at him with its gasoline-lantern eyes. "What do you think the Veil is, Bill?"

"Before you told me that you'd bent space and time I thought it was a space-time warp."

"What do you think it is now?"

"I think it's an interface. I think that when you created a warp between Earth and Alioth Sixteen a time-flux came into being that on this part of Earth brought the past and the future together. And I think that my sled carried Dunyzad and me through the interface because I partially negated the impulse I'd begun to feed into the photon scrambler and brought about an ephemeral equilibrium between the past and the future."

"You're right, Bill—it *is* an interface," Ed-Dimiryat said. "Do you know, I felt from the first moment I saw you that you were intelligent and would more than qualify for service in the computer."

"The *computer?*"

"Yes. You'll be quite happy there, and—"

"Wait a minute," Billings shouted, "I didn't come here to apply for a job—I came here to ask you how I could get back through the Veil. So tell me, and I'll be gone. And don't pretend you don't know how, because I have it from Dunny that Jinn go through it all the time—or used to. Even the thieves know how to get through, not to mention the ghuls."

"The thieves never bother us, so we leave them alone."

"Well I'm not bothering you either."

"Granted, you aren't bothering us, and we have no reason to think you ever will. But that female you brought with you is another matter. She's a troublemaker, and if she finds out how to pass back and forth through the interface she may return and—"

"She's just a kid! Surely you're not afraid of her!"

"She's a menace to our society."

"That's ridiculous!"

"You didn't see the owl on top of the tower, did you? It's a very small one and sits in a niche just above the window. If we Jinn had had any doubts about the female's hostility they were eliminated when she implied she was in possession of the seal of Suleyman. She can't possibly have it, or even have a copy, because it was lost in antiquity. Don't think for one minute that we're afraid of such a silly talisman, because we're not. But we simply can't allow her to go running around bragging she has dominance over the Jinn, either on this side of the interface or the other. And she means to do us physical harm too. No sooner had you entered the tower than she began rummaging through one of the boxes on your vehicle in search of a weapon to use against us. All of us saw her every move, but since the transmitters don't relay video images clearly we were unable to identify the objects she removed from the box. She entered the tower some time ago, your other companion at her heels, but we're prepared for her, of course. Most of the other Jinn are pretending to be asleep in order to lure her deeper into our clutches. At the right moment two 'Efrits will spring upon her. Soon, you will hear her scream. As a matter of fact," Ed-Dimiryat added a little nervously, "she should have screamed already."

Billings pointed his icer at the Marid's midriff. "You guys should feel proud of yourselves, picking on a little girl only a fraction of your size! Either you tell me how to get back through the Veil and agree to leave her alone or I'll turn that smoke you're really made of into a snowstorm!"

Ed-Dimiryat's rock-crusher mouth arced into a grotesque grin. He reached for Billings with one of his mammoth hands. "Perhaps it will be best if I pop you into the computer right now, Bill, and let you get started on your new job."

Stepping back, Billings unloosed a subzero beam and waited for the Marid to turn into snow. There was a loud sputter and a big geyser of steam. When the steam dispersed, there stood the Marid, as unaffected as an elephant hit by a pea.

Billings unloosed two more beams. He got two more geysers, but no snow. By this time Ed-Dimiryat was laughing—if you could call the sound of rocks being ground into dust laughter. "Do you know how this dome and the tower were built, Bill? We Jinn ate copper and zinc and lead and blew them into being!"

Still laughing, it snatched the icer out of Billings' hand and tossed it into its mouth and swallowed it. Then it reached for Billings again. Quickly he dove between its pillarlike legs and headed for the door, forgetting all about his sprained ankle. It brought itself sharply to his attention when he turned it again, and he went sprawling on the floor. Rolling over onto his back, he saw the mammoth hand descending toward him again, and then he saw it stop in midair. A familiar voice said, "In the name of Suleyman Ibn-Da'ud, I command you to desist, you wretched Marid!"

Sitting up, he saw that Dunyzad, her left arm thrust out, had stepped into the room. Behind her stood 'Ali Baba. In one hand he was carrying the self-heating crucible she had asked Billings about and the little ladle he had pointed

out to her, and in the other partially depleted
bundle of soldering rods. Smoke arose from the
crucible, indicating that it contained molten
metal.

XII

Suleyman's Seal

Billings got to his feet and limped over to where Dunyzad was standing. "Stand back, Bill!" she cried, her eyes fixed on Ed-Dimiryat. Her chin was thrust out and there was a belligerent expression on her face. "I am going to teach this wretched Marid a lesson!"

"No, Dunny! You and 'Ali make a run for it. I'll try to hold this monster off as long as I can and maybe you can make it back to the carpet. You never should have left it in the first place!"

She walked right by him, 'Ali Baba just behind her, and halted a short distance from Ed-Dimiryat's huge feet. Not knowing what else to do, Billings followed. He saw that Ed-Dimiryat's gasoline-lantern eyes were locked on the ring on her finger. She raised her arm so that the Marid could see it better. "It is the seal of Suleyman Ibn-Da'ud, Marid!"

"It is not!" Ed-Dimiryat screamed, his words coming through in Arabic. "The seal was lost in antiquity. There's no way you could have obtained a copy."

Dunyzad gazed fearlessly up into the Marid's face. "Detach your brass bottle and set it on the floor," she said.

To Billings' amazement, the Marid obeyed her command. Its eyes had begun to flicker, as though they were running out of gasoline. They were still fixed on the ring.

"Condense yourself," Dunyzad commanded, "and get into the bottle so that I may stopper it with lead and affix the seal of Suleyman!"

The Marid kneeled on the floor before her and clasped its hands together. "Spare me, damsel," it cried. "I am one of the good Jinn. In the Great Battle which Suleyman waged against the Jinn I fought on his side!"

"I do not believe you are one of the good Jinn."

"But I am! After all the heretical Jinn were captured and imprisoned in brass bottles and thrown into the Sea of El-Karkar, Suleyman said to me, 'You are free, Ed-Dimiryat. Take the other good Jinn with you and return to your own land.' "

"I still do not believe you are one of the good Jinn," Dunyzad said. "Get into the bottle!"

"No, no!" Ed-Dimiryat pleaded. "Spare me, spare me, please! I will do anything you ask! I

will enrich you forever! I will build you a palace out of brass! I will grant you three wishes! I
will be your slave for life!"

Dunyzad was inexorable. "Get into the bottle,
wretched creature! Get into it at once!"

"But you will burn me with the hot lead!"

"How can hot lead burn someone who is
made of fire? Do as I command!"

Not once had the Marid moved its gaze from
the ring. Its eyes, Billings saw, had lost most of
their luminescence. As he watched, the huge
torso turned into smoke. (He knew it wasn't
really smoke, but what else could you call it?
Certainly it wasn't sand, the substance he had
at first thought Jinn were made out of, and it
definitely wasn't dust.) The hands and the arms
followed, then the pillarlike legs and the corner-
stone-feet. Finally the domelike head. Then the
smoke began to swirl and to contract. *Hum-
hum-hum*, it went, *hum-hum-hum*, and the
smell of shorted wires filled the rotunda.

Narrower and narrower the cloud of smoke
became, attenuating itself till it almost reached
the highest point of the ceiling. Then it moved
above the bottle and began inching itself down
through the neck. When at last the final tendril
disappeared, Dunyzad took the crucible and
the ladle from 'Ali Baba and went over to the
bottle and began ladling molten solder into the
neck. It was a small neck, and she only needed
three ladlefuls to seal it. She waited till the

solder started to harden; then, standing on her tiptoes, she pressed the seal of her ring against the stopper. "There!"

'Ali Baba was looking at her with admiring eyes. "Is she not remarkable, Emir Bill? Is she not the most remarkable girl you have ever seen in all your life?"

"I—I guess she is," Billings said.

Dunyzad rejoined them and handed 'Ali Baba the ladle and the crucible. "We are all set now, Bill."

"But Dunny, the tower is filled with Jinn! They were hiding in their bottles when I came down the ramp, but they must have come out of them by this time and are probably laying for us."

"No, they are still in them, Bill, and now they cannot get out because I stood on 'Ali's shoulders and filled all the necks with lead and affixed the seal of Suleyman. Two 'Efrits tried to jump us on the ramp, though, and I had to make them get back into their bottles first. So the Jinn will not bother us any more, Bill. 'Long have they ate and drank; but now, after pleasant eating, they themselves have been eaten.' "

Billings just gaped at her. No wonder Ed-Dimiryat had been scared! "Dunny, let me see that ring."

When she held out her hand he took it in his and looked down at the seal. As she had said, it was made of both iron and brass, the iron forming a circlet around the brass. Upon the surface of the brass there was a relief of tiny black Arabic letters. No, not a relief, for the letters appeared to be made of iron. Whoever had made the seal must have fused them to the brass. The words they formed were probably Suleyman's commands to the good and the bad Jinn, but he didn't know Arabic well enough to tell and the letters were so tiny he had to strain his eyes to see them.

But he was far less interested in what the words said than in the geometric figure they formed. He let go of Dunyzad's hand and told her to hold it out with her fingers bent downward so that he could see the seal; then he stopped back several paces. The figure stood out clearly, even from a distance. It consisted of two overlapped equilateral triangles—

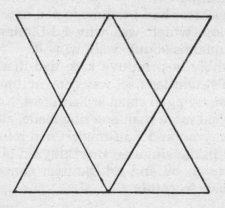

—and the original figure from which Dunyzad had said it had been copied could have been the forerunner of the Star of David.

He discovered that it had an hypnotic effect even upon him. But its effect upon the Jinn went beyond mere hypnosis. It reduced them to jelly. Nevertheless, he knew that the over-lapped triangles alone weren't responsible, that the iron they were made of had contributed to the effect. Dunyzad had said that the Jinn dreaded iron, and he knew now that this must be true. They dreaded it so much, in fact, that they were unable to break through a flimsy stopper which had been stamped with an iron seal.

He understood now why the Jinn in the tower had not attacked Dunyzad and 'Ali Baba while they were still on the time sled. The sled, although mostly made of lightweight metals, had many steel parts.

Billings' icer had been made of a new aluminum alloy, which was why Ed-Dimiryat had had no qualms about swallowing it.

Incredibly, a primitive king had discovered the Jinn's Achilles heel way back in time when they were trying to conquer Earth past. No doubt he had had more than one ring made, although both Dunyzad and Ed-Dimiryat had referred to the seal in the singular. But Dunyzad only had legend to go by and Ed-Dimiryat conceivably could have forgotten.

It had been a long, long time ago.

Billings found it hard to believe the Marid could be that old. Perhaps it had lied about being in the Great Battle. He returned to Dunyzad's side. "Dunny, do you think Ed-Dimiryat *really* fought in the Great Battle?"

She had noticed for the first time that he was limping. "Bill, you hurt your ankle again!"

"It's all right for now. Do you think Ed-Dimiryat *really* fought in the Battle?"

"All of the Jinn did."

"But it was so long ago."

"It must be that Jinn live a long time."

Maybe, Billings thought, it only seems like a long time to us because we live only a short time. "Why are you so certain Ed-Dimiryat wasn't one of the good Jinn?"

"I am not really certain, Bill. But it was attacking you, and that was enough for me."

"Its bottle is a good place for it. I wish, though," Billings said, "that I'd thought to ask you to make it tell us how to get back through the Veil before you made it get inside."

"It can hear through the bottle. I will make it tell us now." She was looking at the big bank of screens. "What are all those little windows, Bill?"

"Come on, I'll show you. You, too, 'Ali. Leave the crucible and that other stuff on the floor."

He pulled himself up to the top of the console and helped them to pull themselves up beside him. "You can see some of the screens better now."

Dunyzad gasped. "Look at those little tiny people! And they are alive? But how can they be so small, Bill?"

He tried to explain that the people weren't really there, that they and their rooms were televised images, but naturally he got nowhere. So he said that the Jinn had employed a special kind of magic to make the people and the rooms seem small.

"What are those little wires on their heads?" 'Ali Baba asked.

"They're thinking," Billings explained. "All of them together. And the wires relay their thoughts to this big box we're standing on. They're extremely smart. They are, in fact, the smartest of all the prisoners, which is why they are in those windows. When the Jinn wanted something added up, they asked them to do it, and when they had a question they didn't know the answer to, they asked them. And what we're going to do, 'Ali and Dunny, is set them and all the other prisoners free."

Dunyzad's eyes were sparkling. "Bill, before we set the ones in the window free we should make them tell us first how to get back through the Veil. If they are so smart, they certainly must be much smarter than Ed-Dimiryat. And they will be so grateful that we are going to set them free that they will not lie to us the way Ed-Dimiryat might.''

Now why didn't *I* think of that? Billings thought.

There was only one problem: how did you go about asking a group of people a question when there was no way you could ask it?

But maybe he could find a way.

XIV
The Cerebralites

"To let them out," 'Ali Baba said, "all we will need to do is break the windows and then catch them when they jump down. They will then resume their normal size, will they not, Emir Bill?"

Billings looked at him. Oh well, he thought. "Right now, 'Ali, the problem is how we can communicate with them."

"Maybe if we shout loud enough they will hear us."

"But the rooms may be a long ways away," Dunyzad said. "Just because they seem to be up there on the wall does not mean they are really there."

"They *look* like they are really there."

"But that does not mean that they are."

Billings had knelt down and was examining

the control board. Logic had already told him that the solitary screen must be a readout screen. It had told him as well that the Cerebralites, not the Jinn, were the authors of the entire electronic setup; that they had, in effect, dug the hole they were now buried in.

It had also apprised him that, aside from the tower and the dome, they and the rest of the people whom the Jinn were "rehabilitating" had built the entire city and the wall which surrounded it.

Kneeling, he looked at the control board's only keyboard. It could be called such only because it had two keys instead of one. Neither was marked. To the left of them was a series of narrow foot-long slots spaced about an eighth of an inch apart. He knew he must be looking at a built-in microphone. He leaned over it. "Hey," he said, then looked at the readout screen. It remained empty.

He returned his attention to the keyboard. But was it a keyboard? Maybe the "keys" were switches. He pushed the left-hand one down. "Hey," he said into the mike again. The readout screen still remained empty.

He pushed the right-hand one down and said, "Hey," into the mike again. This time the screen lighted up and words appeared: MESSAGE INCOMPREHENSIBLE.

Dunny read the words too. "Bill, they answered in Arabic."

The words he was looking at were English. But there was no need to bother his head about the discrepancy with a human computer at his fingertips. "What language are you speaking in?" he asked.

ALL LANGUAGES.

"How is that possible?"

BY THE USE OF THOUGHT-WORDS. WHO ARE YOU?

"We are three people from the land of Men who have imprisoned Ed-Dimiryat and the rest of the Jinn in bottles and who wish to free you."

PUSH THE BLUE BUTTON! PUSH THE BLUE BUTTON! PUSH THE BLUE BUTTON! IT IS AN ON-OFF SWITCH WHICH WILL EXTINGUISH THE BLUE LIGHT!

"Where is it?"

THERE IS A LITTLE CAP FLUSH WITH THE SURFACE OF THE CONTROL BOARD JUST ABOVE THE READOUT SCREEN. RAISE IT.

Billings found the cap and raised it. Sure enough, there was a blue button underneath. "All right, I've found it."

PUSH IT, PUSH IT, PUSH IT!

Dunyzad was looking at the screens on the display board. "They are excited, Bill. One of them is jumping up and down."

"Before I push the button," Billings said, "I want you to do us a favor."

NAME IT, NAME IT, NAME IT!

"When I and one of my companions came through the Veil—the interface—we did so accidentally and now we don't know how to get back through. Tell us how and I'll set you free."

WE DO NOT TRUST YOU! YOU MUST FREE US FIRST!

"You can tell us how, can't you?"

OF COURSE WE CAN! WE ARE GENIUSES! THERE IS NOTHING WE DO NOT KNOW! BUT BEFORE WE TELL YOU YOU MUST SET US FREE. PUSH THE BUTTON, PUSH THE BUTTON, PUSH THE BUTTON!

"How will just turning out the light set them free, Bill?" Dunyzad asked.

"It's a magic light that makes it impossible for them to free themselves—they and all the other people in the city." He leaned back over the mike. "Do you promise to tell us how?"

CROSS OUR HEARTS AND HOPE TO DIE! CROSS OUR HEARTS AND HOPE TO DIE!

He looked at Dunyzad, wondering how the thought words had come out in Arabic. He didn't need to ask her, for she said, "They swear by Allah, Bill."

"Do you think we can trust them?"

"I do not know. The ones I looked at through the windows have mean faces."

"How about you, 'Ali?"

"I think we will have to, Emir Bill."

"Well, they're people and we're people," Billings said, "so I guess in a way we're obligated to take them at their word."

"I guess we do not have much choice, Bill," Dunyzad said.

He spoke into the mike again. "When we free you, come to the dome."

WE WILL BE THERE. WE WILL BE THERE. PUSH THE BUTTON, PUSH THE BUTTON, PUSH THE BUTTON!

Billings pushed it. He had an uncanny feeling that he had made a mistake even before the first Cerebralite came barging through a doorway that, an instant ago, had been part of the rotunda wall.

Remembering his manners, Billings lowered himself from the console and limped forward to greet the new arrival. The Cerebralite was at least seven feet tall, had broad shoulders, Herculean muscles and ugly little brown eyes. He walked right by Billings as though Billings didn't exist and went over and kicked the brass bottle Ed-Dimiryat was imprisoned in.

Other Cerebralites poured into the room. There were brown ones, white ones, black ones and yellow ones. All of them, even the females, were at least seven feet tall, and all of them looked like participants in a body builders' contest. Every one of them ignored Billings and went over and kicked the brass bottle.

"By Allah, they are big!" he heard 'Ali Baba exclaim.

By this time the rotunda was filled with them.
They formed a big circle around the brass bottle,
clasped hands and began to dance around it as
though it were a Maypole. As they danced,
they sang a little song. In English, the words
came out as follows:

"Good-bye to you, Ed,
We're glad that you're back in your bottle;
We've taken over your Kingdom,
And all of us hope that you throttle!"

Billings pulled himself back up on top of the
console. "I—I do not think they like Ed-Dimiryat
very much," Dunyzad said.

"I guess they kind of have it in for it."

'Ali Baba's face was pale. "It—it is lucky it is
safe in its bottle."

The sound of a scream came through the
doorway by which the Cerebralites had entered
the rotunda. It was followed by another. By
this time the streets were probably filled with
the newly liberated prisoners. Looking at the
dancers, Billings was shocked to see that the
women were taking off their tunics.

More screams came from the streets.

Talk about Pandora!

"Hey!" he shouted at the dancers. "Hey!"

Gradually their rhythmic side-step came to a
halt, and one by one they faced him. "You
people made a promise!" he said, speaking in

Arabic so Dunyzad and 'Ali could keep abreast of what was going on. "Aren't you going to keep it?"

The Cerebralites looked at one another. Presently they began to laugh. The laughter reverberated throughout the rotunda and sounded almost as bone-chilling as Ed-Dimiryat's had. Then they came milling over to the console. "What promise is he talking about?" one of them said to the others in a loud voice.

"You know what promise!" Billings shouted. "You agreed to tell us how to get back through the Veil if we freed you! So tell us!"

"Veil?" The word was tossed about among the bald heads. "What Veil?"

"You know what Veil!"

"You have no business even being here, you wretched pygmies!" one of the Cerebralites suddenly shouted. "This is *our* building!"

Another shout: "Let's feed them to the *ghuls!*"

"No, to the rukhs!"

"No! Let's throw them into the streets and let the savages take care of them!"

A Cerebralite reached out and tried to grab Billings' ankle. He took a half step back. The throng milled closer to the Console. It had turned into a mob.

What was he going to do?"

"Throw them into the streets! Throw them into the streets!"

Dunyzad stepped forward. Placing her hands

on her hips, she said, "How were you people able to fit in those little rooms? They will not contain either your hands or your feet—how, then, could they have contained all of you?"

Get back, Dunny, Billings started to say, and then he saw that the Cerebralites were staring at her. "You don't *believe* we were in them?" one of them asked.

"I will never believe you were in them till I see you in them!"

"But you *did* see us in them!"

"All I saw were people as little as mice. You people are the size of elephants!"

Smug expressions began to show on the Cerebralites' faces. Here was someone so intellectually inferior to them that she didn't know that images could be broadcast by radiowaves into tiny picture tubes! Here was a golden opportunity to show her how smart they were and how dumb she was!

Nevertheless, Billings didn't believe for one instant that they would bite on Dunyzad's bait. The Cerebralites were geniuses, and even though they had been behaving like a bunch of vengeful kids, deep down inside they were cool, levelheaded thinkers. No, they would never—

"SHOW HER, SHOW HER, SHOW HER!" the shout went up, and as he stood there staring, they began filing out of the rotunda.

"Wave to us so we can be sure you are there," Dunyzad called after them.

In a few minutes she, Billings and 'Ali Baba had the big room all to themselves.

They turned and looked at the lower screens. Billings did not believe it when he saw tiny men and women entering the tiny rooms and attaching electrodes and wires to the tops of their heads. They then sat down at their tables and began to wave. Pretty soon there were flutterings in almost all of the screens. Looking at the console screen, Billings saw the words, THERE, WE ARE ALL BACK IN OUR LITTLE ROOMS. NOW DO YOU BELIEVE, DAMSEL? NOW DO YOU BELIEVE?

Billings pushed the blue button.

Silence fell upon the city.

The admiration which had taken up permanent residence in 'Ali Baba's soft brown eyes was now tinged with awe. He stepped closer to Billings. "Is she not remarkable, Emir Bill? Is she not the most remarkable girl you have ever seen in all your life?"

"I—I guess she is," Billings said.

XV

Young Love

"I guess you know, Dunny," Billings said, "that we've got to set the Jinn free."

She nodded. "But before we do so I am going to make the Marid tell us how to get back through the Veil. And before I do that I am going to take care of your ankle."

She and Billings and 'Ali Baba had lowered themselves back down to the rotunda floor. She made Billings sit down, and unwound and then rewound the bandage on his ankle, making it much tighter. "See if you can put all your weight on that foot now, Bill."

He found that he could. They joined 'Ali Baba, who had gone over to the brass bottle and was looking at it closely. "It is incredible how such a great big Jinni can fit in there, Emir Bill."

It wasn't incredible to Billings, because he

knew that the solidity of all objects, animate or inanimate, is an illusion, but he still couldn't understand how a living creature could collapse its own molecular structure or how it could alter its outward appearance, and he knew that he never would.

Dunyzad tapped on the bottle. "Ed-Dimiryat?"

"I am here, damsel."

"We have decided to set you and the other Jinn free, because it has become evident to us that the people in the city are even more despicable than the Jinn are and need someone to watch over them. But there is something you are going to have to tell us first."

"I think I know what it is you wish to know, damsel."

"In case you do not, I will inform you: we wish to know how we can get back through the Veil."

"There's a hiatus in the interface which you can pass through."

"A what?"

"He means a hole, Dunny," Billings said. "Where is it?" he asked Ed-Dimiryat.

"To the west of the mountains."

"The whole desert is west of the mountains!"

"To be exact, it's directly west of the mountain which stands at the foot of the valley. The mountain where the thieves' cave is. You won't be able to see the hiatus of course, but it's a wide one, and if you proceed due west from the mountain peak, there's an excellent chance you'll pass through it on the first try."

"Is that how the Jinn go through the Veil?"

"No. Lacking your rigid molecular structure, we can pass through it at any point."

"One more question," Billings said. "Why did the Jinn try to conquer Earth past?"

"We weren't trying to conquer Earth past! That dumb king just thought we were! We only went there to get copper. This phase of Earth is almost devoid of it. We were going to build a big brass city to which we could go for rest and relaxation now and then while we were rehabilitating the terrestrials. But that dumb king went and got a whole army together and somehow he found out about our one and only weakness. But most of us escaped, and regardless of what he may have said afterward, he only managed to imprison one or two Jinn in brass bottles."

"You told me before that you were one of the good Jinn and that you fought on Suleyman's side!" Dunyzad exclaimed. "And how dare you refer to Suleyman Ibn-Da'ud as a dumb king!"

"Hush, Dunny," Billings said. "It was only trying to placate you before by going along with the legend. At least it's leveling with us now. After you finish rehabilitating this last batch of people what are you going to do?" he asked the Marid.

"We're going home! We've had enough of this wretched planet. We'll turn it over to the *ghuls!*"

Billings looked at Dunyzad. "I guess that's about it, Dunny. Should we start pulling the stoppers out?"

"But what did the Marid mean when it said they were going home, Bill? I thought that this was their home."

"No. They're from another world. You've got to stretch your mind a little to understand, Dunny. You too, 'Ali. Way up there in the sky there are other worlds. The Jinn came from one of them."

They regarded him for some time. Then 'Ali Baba said, "How?"

"They made the distance between their world and this one much shorter by bending space."

"But space cannot be bent," 'Ali Baba said. "And even if it could be, how would it be possible to get hold of it?"

"All it is," Dunyzad said, "is empty air."

"You can't explain it to them!" Ed-Dimiryat shouted. "Let me out of here!"

"You shut up!" Billings said. "What I was trying to say, Dunny, was that when you bend space between two different points you can cover the distance between them in a single step instead of having to walk miles and miles and miles. But even when space is bent in such a manner, the real distance remains the same to the observer, and so their world is still as far away from this one as it was in the first place. Do you see what I mean now, Dunny? Do you, 'Ali?"

Two blank stares. At length Dunyzad said, "Is the world of the Jinn farther away than the fixed stars?"

He remembered that in the ninth century Ptolemy still ruled the astronomical roost. The Ptolemaic cosmography consisted of eight spheres, the eighth of which comprised the "fixed stars," but later astronomers had added two more. The tenth sphere—the primum mobile— constituted the edge of the universe, so he guessed he'd better settle for the "fixed stars." "No, it's no farther away than they are."

"Then if it is a great big world like this one, we should be able to see it," 'Ali Baba said.

"Bill, you're wasting your time!" Ed-Dimiryat shouted. "Let me out of here!"

"It's just too far away for us to see it, 'Ali."

"But we can see the fixed stars," Dunyzad said.

"I think," Billings said a little desperately, "that it's probably behind one of them."

"But they are so small, Emir Bill! How could one of them hide a whole world?"

"They aren't really that small. They just look small from here." He could tell from his pupils' faces that he had gotten absolutely nowhere. "Just take my word for it that it's up there somewhere—all right?"

"We know that it is there if you say so, Emir Bill.'"

"Good. Let's get busy and free the Jinn."

He pulled out his jackknife, opened it and pried out the stopper from Ed-Dimiryat's bottle. Then 'Ali Baba picked up the crucible and the ladle and the bundle of soldering rods—miraculously, none of the three items had been stomped on by the Cerebralites—and they left the Marid brooding in the rotunda and reentered the tower. In each of the rooms Billings had Dunyzad stand on his shoulders and undo the work she had done. The Jinn must have been demoralized, for none of them came out of their bottles.

The time sled hovered exactly where Billings had parked it. He boarded it and helped Dunyzad and 'Ali make the step from the window ledge to the deck. 'Ali replaced the crucible and the ladle and the soldering rods in the toolbox and closed and sat down on the lid. Dunyzad and Billings belted themselves in their seats and Billings set the craft in motion.

"We are going to the cave for the treasure first, aren't we, Bill?" Dunyzad asked.

Billings had stopped kidding himself. He had been poor all his life through no fault of his own. His mother and father had been poor all their lives too, and so had his grandparents on both sides. Here, at last, at his very fingertips, lay an opportunity to change this sorry genealogical scheme of things once and for all. "You bet we are," he said.

*   *   *

The moon had set and only the gentle light of the stars illumined the valley. The orchards and fields had become pale ghosts of themselves, the stream an anfractuous apparition.

The adventure had almost come to an end. Soon Billings would be able to take Dunyzad on a round trip to the twenty-first century and the sense of responsibility that lay so heavily upon his shoulders would vanish. He should have felt relieved; instead, he felt awful. The big lie he had told her lay like lead upon his thoughts and it grew heavier with each passing moment. He wanted to get rid of it by telling her the truth, but he did not dare. Not because he might lose his job if Animanikins, Inc. got wind of his apostasy but because he dreaded the look that would come into her eyes. And the fact that she had saved him from the thieves and from the Jinn made it all the more difficult for him to disillusion her.

How could he tell her the truth anyway when 'Ali Baba was leaning so far forward from his seat on the toolbox that his nose was almost touching her hair, and would hear every word he said?

"I smell flowers!" she exclaimed suddenly. "Do you, Bill?"

He became aware that the scent was all around him. It overpowered the traces of nedd which still lingered in her hair. He identified it as jasmine, but he knew that jasmine was only the

predominant fragrance, that other scents were
involved.

He looked over the edge of the sled. So did
Dunyzad and 'Ali Baba. They were passing over
a field, but it was different from the other fields
in the valley. It was covered with parterres,
pale paths winding among them.

It must be a flower garden, Billings thought.

"The flowers must be beautiful if they are as
beautiful as they smell," Dunyzad said. "I want
to pick some, Bill."

"I do too," 'Ali Baba said.

So did Billings—why, he did not know. There
was no great hurry to get back to the cave, so
why not give in to the impulse? He eased up
on the anti-grav, knowing in the back of his
mind that he would have given in to the impulse whether he had wanted to or not.

The sled drifted downward and the fragrance
rose up to meet it. The scene was so overpow-
ering now that it was almost tangible. He guided
the sled toward a path between two of the
parterres and brought it gently to the ground.
The parterres rose up on either side, emitting
their lovely scent, but he could discern no
flowers.

And then he saw the g*huls*.

They leaped out of the "parterres" upon the
sled. There were five of them, grotesque, foul-
smelling, their bodies covered with the dark
blotches of sores. The creation of the illusion

must have sapped their hypnotic powers, leaving them none left over for themselves. Two of them seized 'Ali Baba and pulled him from the sled. The others grabbed Dunyzad and Billings, but they could not budge them because of the seat belts. 'Ali Baba struggled fiercely but could not escape. Billings managed to push his and Dunyzad's attackers from the sled. He assessed his opportunities both from a present and future standpoint, made a quick decision and jammed tho emergency time-jump key down.

The starlight blinked, the ghuls and 'Ali Baba vanished, and Dunyzad and Billings found themselves sitting alone on the sled in tho middle of a field covered with scattered piles of brushwood.

"Where is 'Ali, Bill? Where is 'Ali? And where are the ghuls?"

"It's all right, Dunny. I jumped us ahead in time. The way I did yesterday morning when the rukh tried to grab us when we were trying to reach the cave."

"But they will kill and eat him!" Her voice held a note of hysteria and the starlight revealed the distress in her eyes. "We should not have run away! We should have stayed and fought them!"

"Easy, Dunny—we're going to jump back and save him."

He unfastened his safety belt, opened the

toolbox and felt for and found a 12″ crescent
wrench. He cursed Ed-Dimiryat for having eaten
his icer. He found a ball-peen hammer and
handed it to Dunyzad. Then he leaned over the
control board and looked at the emergency time-
jump dial, which glowed with its own light. It
was still set at the maximum fifteen-minute
setting he had used when he eluded the rukh.
He set it back one minute and changed the
directional lock from *plus* to *minus*. A coincidence would be impossible, since temporal motion precluded tangibility.

"When we reappear, Dunny, we'll only have
been missing one minute, and the *ghuls* will be
as surprised to see us as they must have been
when we vanished. I'll jump the two who
grabbed 'Ali—they can't have moved very far
away—and by the time they and the others
have gotten over their surprise I'll have freed
him. You stay on the carpet and use that hammer if any of them try to grab you. And don't,
whatever you do, unfasten that belt!"

She had calmed down a little. "All right,
Bill."

"All set to go?"

"All set."

He pushed the key back down.

The illusion of the flower garden had already
faded away, and the field, except for the presence of 'Ali Baba and the *ghuls*, was no differ-

ent from the one they had just "left." As Billings
had anticipated, a second wave of surprise swept
over the ghuls. It swept over 'Ali Baba too,
judging from the size of his eyes.

The two ghuls who had grabbed him had
stepped a short ways back from where they
had been before and pulled him with them.
The other ghuls had stepped a short ways back
also. Leaping from the sled, Billings rushed the
two who held 'Ali. He knocked one of them to
his knees with a blow from the wrench, pulled
'Ali free from the other and shoved him toward
the sled. He was about to follow when one of
the other ghuls jumped upon his back and bore
him to the ground. He twisted around and
swung the wrench again. The ghul collapsed
and Billings rolled from underneath him and
got to his feet. At this point he found himself
confronted by the most beautiful woman he
had ever seen in his whole life.

"Come," she whispered, holding out her arms.
"Come to me."

Her lips, even in the starlight, were a flaming
red. Her long black hair fanned out over her
bare shoulders. The filmy dress that cascaded
from her breasts to the midway point of her
thighs was only one whit less transparent than
the light of the stars. He felt as though he were
falling into the liquid depths of her eyes.

"Come to me," she whispered again. "Come
to me."

He took a step forward. He was about to take another, but did not, for Dunyzad, who had crept up behind her, brained her with the ball-peen hammer. She turned into a hideous hag and fell to the ground.

The two remaining g*huls* ran away. *Dunny,* he started to say, still half in a daze, *I told you to stay on the carpet!* And then he saw that she had thrown her arms around 'Ali Baba's neck.

" 'Ali, 'Ali—are you all right?"

"Oh yes, I am fine," 'Ali Baba said, and put his arms around her waist.

Young love. There was nothing more beautiful on this Earth or on the Earth of long ago. Ali's hair was as long as hers was, and no less pleasing to the eye. The starlight fondled their youthful faces as though it, too, knew that these two beautiful teenagers had become one. The night seemed to fawn at their feet.

Billings kicked the time sled as hard as he could. Fortunately he remembered to use his left foot. "All right, you two," he said. "Break it up and let's go!"

XVI

Exit Dunny

The lamp which Billings had left on in the outer chamber had not run out of oil, and the mouth of the cave looked like a big window on the dark mountainside. When he guided the sled through it he kept one finger on the emergency time-jump key, the directional lock of which he had changed from *minus* to *plus*, but there was no sign of either the thieves or their horses.

He led the way through the tunnel, shining the beam of his flashlight before him. The lamps in the treasure chamber were still burning too. Soon, though, they would run out of oil, but by then the "three thieves" would be gone. Billings had written off the gold ingots, and he told Dunyzad and 'Ali Baba to forget about them too, and the silver ingots as well. However tempting the gold might be, the ingots were just plain too heavy to fool around with, and the sled hadn't been built to carry very much weight, but even if it had been it would have been foolish for him to return to the twenty-first century with a pile of gold ingots in plain sight because the museum would have snatched them right out from under his nose.

So the "three thieves" concentrated on the jewels instead, filling their pockets with them. 'Ali Baba asked Billings if he could fill some of the *kullehs* too, and Billings told him to go ahead. Billings already had enough in his pockets to make him rich. For the most part, the jewels consisted of gold and silver anklets and bracelets, which were embellished with rubies or diamonds or emeralds or lapis lazuli, gold rings set with similar precious gems, gold and silver earrings and pearl necklaces. In the twenty-first century those that Billings had taken would be worth ten times their real value because they had been made in the ninth.

Dunyzad finished filling the pockets of her bloomers. She had also taken possession of the "Lamp of the Aesthetic." She and Billings watched 'Ali Baba as he filled the *kullehs*. He had lined all of them up and was scooping jewels into them with one of the big earthenware cups the thieves had drunk their *buzah* from. "He really wants to be rich," Billings said.

"That is because he is rich already. Rich people like to be richer."

"But you're rich too."

"Well, my father is not poor."

"The way you talked before, you were going to load up the whole carpet."

"I was thinking of the gold and silver ingots, and you said not to take them. Besides," she said, "with the 'Lamp of the Aesthetic' I do not need a lot of treasure. And anyway, I am taking something else back of even more value."

"All I saw you put in your pockets were jewels."

"The treasure I referred to is my head. It is the story of our adventure, which I am going to tell Sheherazade as soon as I go to see her. Just think of all the ideas she will get for tales to tell the Sultan! She has already made up lots of stories about the Jinn and once she made one up about ghuls. But now her horizon will be expanded, Bill. For instance, think of what a wonderful story she will be able to make up about the treasure cave and the forty thieves and 'Ali Baba!"

"But there were only fourteen thieves."

"Oh, there were more than that!"

Billings decided not to argue. At least he knew now where Sheherazade had gotten the idea for " 'Ali Baba and the Forty Thieves." Probably when she saw the "Lamp of the Aesthetic" and Dunyzad told her about Dahish, she would invent "The Story of Aladdin and the Wonderful Lamp."

"Do you ever help your sister make up stories, Dunny?" he asked.

"Sometimes."

"It must be fun."

"It is. But what I do mainly though," Dunyzad said, "is try to make her stick to facts whenever the story we are making up is based on real life."

Billings just looked at her.

'Ali Baba had finished filling the *kullehs*. "There, I think that these will be enough, Emir Bill."

"There are six more on the magic carpet," Billings said cynically.

"No. I do not wish to seem greedy."

"Let's go then."

Dunyzad turned out the lamps and she and Billings helped 'Ali carry the *kullehs* of jewels through the tunnel and load them on the sled. Outside the cave the first gray light of the new day had begun to drive the darkness away. After Dunyzad and 'Ali climbed on board the sled, Billings turned out the last lamp and got on board himself. He guided the sled out into the dawnlight, rounded the side of the mountain and took an azimuth when the sled was exactly west of the peak.

None of the rukhs were up yet, of if they were, Billings saw no sign of them. He guided the sled over the mountains and the hills and the oases. He hit the hiatus on the first try, but he didn't know it till the oasis-dotted desert transmuted abruptly into a treeless plain with hills showing in the distance.

There were ruins up ahead. "I know where we are!" 'Ali Baba exclaimed. "That is the dead city of Bardaur. The house of my father is beyond those hills."

"Before we go to your palace, Bill," Dunyzad said, "we will have to take 'Ali home."

Did she still want to go to his "palace," he wondered, or was she afraid to tell him she and 'Ali had fallen in love? The question shouldn't have bothered him in the least, since he had no palace to take her to, but it did. Probably because he was tired and couldn't think straight. "Show us the way, 'Ali."

Although 'Ali Baba was rich now, the farm of his father did not indicate he had been rich before. The house was small, and built of clay bricks. There were only two other buildings, both of which were also built of clay bricks and one of which appeared to be a stable. There were lots of chickens, though, and plenty of goats.

His parents, when they saw the "magic carpet," gasped, and so did his older brother Kasim. They fell all over Dunyzad but looked at Billings with a trace of awe in their eyes.

Their eyes got big when they saw the *kullehs* of jewels, and they helped 'Ali carry them into the house. Billings emptied the water out of the six *kullehs* he had filled and carried them in too, in order to get rid of them, and Dunyzad brought in the cantaloupes to abet the breakfast which 'Ali's mother had already set about preparing.

During breakfast 'Ali narrated their adventures in the land of the Jinn. Nine-tenths of what he said had to do with Dunyzad. He described in detail how she had danced to throw the thieves off guard and how she had rubbed the "Lamp of the Aesthetic" and brought Dahish to their rescue, and he described how she had imprisoned the Jinn in their brass bottles and how she had tricked the "window people" into reentering their tiny rooms. All the while he talked he kept glancing at Dunyzad, and his eyes glowed with the idolatrous light which sooner or later illumines the eyes of most young men.

After breakfast he dumped the *kullehs* on the floor and added the contents of his pockets to the big pile of jewels. His parents and his brother seated themselves in a circle around it and started taking inventory. Their eyes glittered as brightly as the jewels in the pile. 'Ali Baba left them to their task and took Dunyzad and Billings on a tour of the farm. He let Dunyzad feed the chickens and afterward he showed her and

Billings his goats. Again he related how he had raised poor Bedr-el-Budur from a kid, and tears came into his eyes. Tears came into Dunyzad's too. Billings gritted his teeth. The last thing in the world he had needed was another rundown of the life and times of Bedr-el-Budur. Not only was he tired, but he needed a shave, and felt terrible. And the big lie he had told Dunyzad had grown so large in his mind it had turned into an ingot.

"Dunny," he said finally, "I think it's time we should go."

He couldn't tell from her eyes, which were wet with tears for Bedr-el-Budur, whether she wanted to leave or not, but he was certain his "palace" had lost its lure, and that she would fur rather remain on the farm and feed the chickens again. But all she said was, "Whenever you are ready, Bill."

They said good-bye to 'Ali and his parents and his brother. Again there were tears in 'Ali's eyes, but this time they were not for his goat. "Now that you know where I live, Dunyzad," he said, "perhaps you will come and visit me."

"Oh, I will, 'Ali. I will."

He looked at Billings. Then he looked at the sled. He sighed. "Somehow I do not think so."

She handed him the "Lamp of the Aesthetic." "Here, this will prove I will come. But you must take good care of it for me till I come and get it, and promise not to rub it."

"I promise, Dunyzad. Every time I look at it I will see your face." He turned toward Billings. "Goodbye, Emir Bill. I wish to thank you for all you have done for me. Were it not for you, I would not even be alive . . . Good-bye, Dunyzad."

The kid is for real, Billings thought. Dunny couldn't have done better if she'd tried. It's wonderful that they've fallen in love.

But why did the thought make him so sad?

He lifted the sled and guided it over the hills till the farm was out of sight. He could make the jump to the present any time, and the sooner he did so the better, because he was already over three days late. Why, then, did he hesitate?

He knew why.

He put the sled on hover. "Dunny," he said, "I haven't got a palace."

"Well perhaps your dwelling is not quite big enough to be called a palace, but lots of people call their dwellings palaces when they are nothing of the sort, so that is nothing to be ashamed of, Bill."

"I am not an emir either."

She looked at him but said nothing.

He pointed down to a field below them in which an old man in a burnoose was standing, staring up at the sled. "Do you see that old man? I am as poor as he is."

She peered over the edge of the sled.

"And do you see his house?" Billings went on. "It is even bigger than mine."

The house was the size of a chicken coop and looked a little bit like one. "But Bill—"

"Dunny, listen to me and try to stretch your mind, because what I'm going to tell you will be kind of hard to grasp."

"Very well, I have stretched it, Bill."

He leveled with her. He leveled with her so completely, in fact, that he felt level himself. He described the animanikins as walking, talking dolls. Time travel didn't give him as bad a time as he thought it would, for he had time-jumped the sled twice when she was with him, so she knew that it could be done. The temporal distance he had covered in coming back to the ninth century must have taxed her imagination, but if it did she gave no sign. He told her that most twenty-first-century Americans were so fascinated by very important past people that they loved to watch and listen to walking, talking dolls which looked just like the real thing and were willing to pay any number of dinars for the privilege of doing so. He told her that this was his first assignment and that she was the first past person he had borrowed, and he said that he had been instructed to lie to her but that he probably would have lied to her anyway in order to quiet her down. He went on to say that a doll had already been made of the Sultan and that a room exactly like the one in which her sister told him stories was being built and that the doll museum expected to make a small fortune when people started coming to see the display.

"But I am not an important person," she said. "Why do you need me?" And then, "I know what happened. You came back to borrow Sheherazade and got me by mistake!"

"I—I thought you were her. But we need you too, Dunny, because you're important too. What I want to do is take you to the future first so that a doll can be made of you. It won't hurt you and will only take a little while. Then I'll bring you back and borrow Sheherazade."

"The Sultan said nothing about his being taken to the future."

"It's such a strange experience for a past person that it probably seems like a dream." (He saw no point in mentioning that the Sultan had put up such a struggle that he had to be tranquilized.) "It won't seem like a dream to you, though, if you decide to go, because now you know all about it and will understand what's happening."

She was silent. He looked at her face. She was staring straight ahead and he could only see her profile. It told him nothing. Finally she said, "If I refuse to go with you, will you force me to?"

"No. Whether you go or not is entirely up to you."

"If I do not, you may lose your job."

"I don't care much about my job."

"But you might lose it."

The tone of her voice told him no more than her profile did. He wished he could see into her eyes. He was certain they would reveal whether she despised or merely hated him. "Yes, I might lose it," he said.

"Then I will go."

"Don't go unless you want to, Dunny."

"It sounds like it may be fun. Here, put all my jewels into your pockets, Bill, in case one of the sorcerers tries to steal them."

She began ladling them out. The jewels he already had in his pockets had settled, and he found he had room for hers. "We'll divide them up when I bring you back, Dunny."

She said nothing, but she was facing him now and he could see into her eyes. They made him think of violets growing in the woods in spring but they told him nothing of her thoughts. He sighed. "Hang on, Dunny—here we go."

A moment after the sled and its two occupants popped into view in the museum's Chronochamber two technicians whisked Dunyzad off to the Big Pygmalion room. It was the last Billings saw of her, for a quarter of an hour later the Curator called him over the intercom and told him his services were no longer required. When Billings asked why, the Curator said that he had taken over three days to complete an assignment that at the most should only have required only one, and that he had brought the wrong girl back to boot. Billings argued that the museum would need an animanikin of Dunyzad as well as one of Sheherazade, and that since the exhibit wasn't going to be opened to the public for another six months, three days were little more than a drop in the bucket, but he would have done as well to argue with the moon. He went a little crazy then, and tried to knock down the Big Pygmalion room door. The guards were called and he was dragged out of the building and his street clothes were thrown out after him. Numbly he picked them up and crossed the street to the parking lot, the jewels jingling in his pockets. Dunny's and his. She would think he was a thief now, and since she already knew he was a liar, she would despise him for the rest of her life. Sadly he climbed into his beat-up car and drove home. But since he saw no reason why he should be both sad and poor, he put up a big sign in his front yard with a single word on it—*Collectibles* (he didn't dare spell out exactly what he had to sell) —and waited for the world to beat a path to his door, and when word at last got round to the true nature of his "collectibles," the world did.

Epilogue

Sheherazade had finished relating "The Story of the Porter and the Ladies of Baghdad," and now she began to relate the first of the tales which the story had paved the way to: "The Story of the First Royal Mendicant."

Billings wished again that he had stayed home. But he knew that if he had he would have tuned in the exhibit on his TV set.

His journey back into the past had been inevitable.

He was no longer quite the same Billings he had been six months ago; he had become a playboy. It should be pointed out, however, that as a playboy he differed radically from the norm. When he stopped in bars, he invariably ordered Seven-Up instead of Cutty Sark. When he tried to sit up all night so he could watch the sun rise, he always sat alone and usually fell asleep before eleven o'clock. When he went shopping for Gucci shoes, he often wound up with sneakers. When girls flocked around his red 1960 Mercedes Benz convertible, he invariably cowered behind the wheel. When he drove into the driveway of his Greek Revival Mansion, he always sneaked in the back door instead of strutting in the front. When he spent a weekend in his new *pied à terre*, he never came out of the house till Monday morning.

It could be said that he was a reclusive playboy.

It can be added that although he was no longer poor, he was still sad.

A girl edged between him and the velvet cord that separated the exhibit from the museum floor, and stood in front of him, half blocking his view. People were getting ruder every day! He pretended she wasn't there and tried to listen to Sheherazade's story and the strains of *Scheherazade*, but for some reason the words and the notes went in one ear and out the other.

The pressure of the crowd shoved him closer to the girl. At first when he smelled nedd he thought the decorators had sprayed the exhibit with it to add a further sense of realism to the past scene. Then he realized that the scent came from the girl.

Why in the world was she wearing nedd when *Jeu de Printemps, numéro cinq* was all the rage?

The anachronism angered him. The last thing he wanted to do was to take another trip back in time.

The girl had bobbed black hair and she was wearing a black shift. Apparently she was aware of his existence, for she slightly turned her head and said, "That kid sitting beside the couch—isn't she the most awkward looking creature you ever saw?"

She meant Dunyzad. Billings hadn't dared to look at her and he had to force himself to now. The technicians must have given the real Dunyzad new clothes to wear before they let Big Pygmalion copy her: new bloomers, a new abbreviated melwatah and a new kufiyeh to wear upon her head. Her animanikin looked stunning in them.

"Isn't she?" the girl asked again.

Billings got mad. "She's beautiful!" he said.

"*Beautiful!* You must have something wrong with your eyes."

"Listen," Billings said, "I'm not going to stand here and have you—"

He paused. That voice. So light and airy, and invested with the tinkling of faraway bells. The girl turned toward him then, and he saw her face. The same soft cheeks, although no longer quite so full. The same violet eyes, but deeper than before. The same expressive mouth, but firmer than he remembered. A little girl's face grown up . . .

She smiled at him. "Hello, Bill."

She was almost as tall as he was and her earrings fringed her nightblack hair like tiny stars and there was a touch of lip rouge on her lips, but the roses in her cheeks were her own. "Dunny, it's not you."

"Yes it is. I thought that you'd be here."

"How *can* it be you?"

"Do you know how Transcendent Jinn disappear, Bill? By moving back and forth in time. They're time travelers, the way you were when you were riding on your 'magic carpet.' "

"*Dahish* brought you to the future? But—"

"I didn't think I would ever see you again. Then, after I got the Lamp back from 'Ali Baba, I asked Dahish what I should do, and he told me he could travel in time. I knew it wouldn't solve my problem if you saw me again as a fifteen-year-old girl, so I had him take me to a point in time four years before you delivered me to the museum. If I hadn't, you would be seeing me again as a little girl and have gone right on pretending to yourself and to me that you hadn't fallen in love. But I didn't leave right away because I had to help my sister make up some more stories to tell the Sultan first. I tried to explain to her and to my father the Vizier and to the Sultan where I was going, but I don't think they quite understood. My father had a fit, and so did my mother, and they tried to stop me, but of course they couldn't because they didn't know about the Lamp. But Sheherazade did, and she kind of smiled at me and said she wished it was her you'd borne away instead of me. I'm glad it wasn't."

"But—"

"When you are in possession of the 'Lamp of the Aesthetic,' Bill you have no problems. When I first arrived I found myself in a land so strange it frightened me, but I had Dahish at my command. He protected me and saw to it that I always had money, and taught me your language and acclimated me to the barbaric customs of your bizarre country."

"But you were in love with 'Ali Baba!" Billings finally got out. "And even if you had been in love with me, you wouldn't have been after I told you I was poor."

"Love cannot be measured in dinars. Besides," Dunyzad said brightly, "you are not poor now."

"Partly because I stole your jewels."

"I know you didn't steal them, Bill. The time traveler who took me back told me you'd been fired."

"But 'Ali Baba!"

"I did not care a fig for him. I liked him, but that was all. It was only you, Bill, from the very beginning. I fell in love with you the minute I looked at you after you bore me aloft on your 'magic carpet,' and even though I was just a kid I knew it was the real thing. But of course I kept it to myself. Fifteen-year-old girls aren't supposed to fall in love with mature men, even way back in the ninth century, any more than mature men are supposed to fall in love with fifteen-year-old girls . . . Would you like to take me out to dinner?"

"Right now?"

"Of course right now. I am starved."

They began edging their way through the crowd. "I still don't quite believe it's you," Billings said.

"But it is, Bill. Speaking English and dressed and behaving like an American girl. But my Superjinni quit, and I still have a lot to learn."

"Why did he quit?"

"He got disgusted." They had left the crowd behind them and were walking toward the museum door. "He said he couldn't spend the rest of his stay on Earth catering to just one human being and that he was sick and tired of catering anyway. He demanded the Lamp back, and when I gave it to him he threw it on the floor and stomped on it. He didn't really leave me in the lurch, though, because before he disappeared for good he brought me a bushel basketful of thousand dollar bills."

Billings glanced at her sideways. "Well no, not a bushel basketful," she said, "but a great big bunch of them."

He paused when they reached the door, and she paused beside him. "What made you so sure," he said, "that I was in love with you?"

"I wasn't sure till I saw you kick the 'magic carpet' when I put my arms around 'Ali after we saved him from the *ghuls*."

Billings grinned. "I sort of gave myself away."

"To me, you did, but not to yourself."

Early evening traffic flowed in the street and

the first star had come out. They descended the museum steps and he led the way to the parking lot. It was quiet there, and there was no one around, and he stopped next to his car and kissed her, and she put her arms around his neck and kissed him back. The light from a nearby streetlight touched her face, and looking into her eyes he saw that a springtime breeze had turned the violets in the woods an even sweeter shade of blue.

"Is that your red convertible, Bill?" she cried. "Oh boy!" And they climbed into it and he drove out of the lot and headed for one of the swank restaurants he used to frequent when he was a playboy . . . and they lived together in the utmost happiness for many wondrous and fruitful years till at last they were visited by the terminator of delights and the separator of companions.

END

Note: Chapter III is based on two stories from the Edward W. Lane translation of *The Thousand and One Nights* (published 1839–41). "The Story of the Porter and the Ladies of Baghdad" and "The Story of the Merchant and the Jinni," excerpts from which appear in the text, are from the same translation. In addition, the original spellings of some of the words in the Lane translation have been retained—e.g., "rukh" for "roc," and " 'Efrit" for "afreet."

DAW

DAW BRINGS YOU THESE BESTSELLERS BY
MARION ZIMMER BRADLEY

☐ CITY OF SORCERY	UE1962—$3.50
☐ DARKOVER LANDFALL	UE1906—$2.50
☐ THE SPELL SWORD	UE1891—$2.25
☐ THE HERITAGE OF HASTUR	UE1967—$3.50
☐ THE SHATTERED CHAIN	UE1961—$3.50
☐ THE FORBIDDEN TOWER	UE1894—$3.50
☐ STORMQUEEN!	UE1951—$3.50
☐ TWO TO CONQUER	UE1876—$2.95
☐ SHARRA'S EXILE	UE1988—$3.95
☐ HAWKMISTRESS	UE1958—$3.50
☐ THENDARA HOUSE	UE1857—$3.50
☐ HUNTERS OF THE RED MOON	UE1968—$2.50
☐ THE SURVIVORS	UE1861—$2.95

Anthologies

☐ THE KEEPER'S PRICE	UE1931—$2.50
☐ SWORD OF CHAOS	UE1722—$2.95
☐ SWORD AND SORCERESS	UE1928—$2.95

DAW

The really great fantasy books are
published by DAW:

Andre Norton

- [ ] LORE OF THE WITCH WORLD   UE1750—$2.50
- [ ] HORN CROWN   UE1635—$2.95
- [ ] PERILOUS DREAMS   UE1749—$2.50

C.J. Cherryh

- [ ] THE DREAMSTONE   UE2013—$2.95
- [ ] THE TREE OF SWORDS AND JEWELS   UE1850—$2.95

Lin Carter

- [ ] DOWN TO A SUNLESS SEA   UE1937—$2.50
- [ ] DRAGONROUGE   UE1982—$2.50

M.A.R. Barker

- [ ] THE MAN OF GOLD   UE1940—$3.95

Michael Shea

- [ ] NIFFT THE LEAN   UE1783—$2.95
- [ ] THE COLOR OUT OF TIME   UE1954—$2.50

B.W. Clough

- [ ] THE CRYSTAL CROWN   UE1922—$2.75

DAW

Unforgettable science fiction by DAW's own stars!

M. A. FOSTER

- [ ] THE WARRIORS OF DAWN — UE1994—$2.95
- [ ] THE GAMEPLAYERS OF ZAN — UE1993—$3.95
- [ ] THE MORPHODITE — UE2017—$2.95
- [ ] THE DAY OF THE KLESH — UE2016—$2.95

C.J. CHERRYH

- [ ] 40,000 IN GEHENNA — UE1952—$3.50
- [ ] DOWNBELOW STATION — UE1987—$3.50
- [ ] VOYAGER IN NIGHT — UE1920—$2.95
- [ ] WAVE WITHOUT A SHORE — UE1957—$2.50

JOHN BRUNNER

- [ ] TIMESCOOP — UE1966—$2.50
- [ ] THE JAGGED ORBIT — UE1917—$2.95

ROBERT TREBOR

- [ ] AN XT CALLED STANLEY — UE1865—$2.50

JOHN STEAKLEY

- [ ] ARMOR — UE1979—$3.95

JO CLAYTON

- [ ] THE SNARES OF IBEX — UE1974—$2.75

DAVID J. LAKE

- [ ] THE RING OF TRUTH — UE1935—$2.95

NEW AMERICAN LIBRARY
P.O. Box 999, Bergenfield, New Jersey 07621

Please send me the DAW Books I have checked above. I am enclosing
$_____ (check or money order—no currency or C.O.D.'s).
Please include the list price plus $1.00 per order to cover handling
costs.

Name _____

Address _____

City _____ State _____ Zip Code _____
Please allow at least 4 weeks for delivery

DAW

Do you long for the great novels of high adventure such as Edgar Rice Burroughs and Otis Adelbert Kline used to write? You will find them again in these DAW novels, filled with wonder stories of strange worlds and perilous heroics in the grand old way:

DAW

A GALAXY OF SCIENCE FICTION STARS!